THE WORLD OVER

Edith Wharton, born in New York in 1862, stemmed from and married into America's upper class, of which she became, as a novelist and short story writer, a formidable critic, while remaining staunchly conservative. Wharton was the first woman ever to win the Pulitzer Prize, for *The Age of Innocence.* After a life of ceaseless activity, she died in 1937.

Anthony Gardner contributes articles and book reviews to the *Daily Telegraph, Sunday Times Magazine* and the *Mail on Sunday.* He edits the Royal Society of Literature's annual journal, the *RSL,* and is himself a Fellow.

The World Over

The World Over

———————————

Edith Wharton

FOREWORD BY ANTHONY GARDNER

CAPUCHIN CLASSICS

CAPUCHIN CLASSICS
LONDON

The World Over

© Edith Wharton 1936

This edition published by Capuchin Classics 2012

2 4 6 8 0 9 7 5 3 1

Capuchin Classics
128 Kensington Church Street, London W8 4BH
Telephone: +44 (0)20 7221 7166
Fax: +44 (0)20 7792 9288
E-mail: info@capuchin-classics.co.uk
www.capuchin-classics.co.uk

Châtelaine of Capuchin Classics : Emma Howard

ISBN: 978-1-907429-29-3

Printed and bound by CPI Group (UK) Ltd. Croydon CR0 4YY

CONTENTS

FOREWORD

One hundred and fifty years after her birth, Edith Wharton is remembered chiefly as the author of classic American novels such as *The Age of Innocence* and *The House of Mirth*. But she was also a mistress of the short story, and – like her friend Henry James – an ardent Europhile: settling in France at the end of the First World War, she rarely returned to the USA. It is possible, then, to see the title of this final collection of stories as epitomising her work and itinerant life. Though explored through the eyes of wealthy Americans, the themes she chooses in *The World Over* – first and foremost, the relationship between men and women – are universal. And while five of the seven tales are set in her home country, all contain characters with broader horizons ready to set sail for another continent if required.

In the first story, however, the travellers come in the opposite direction. *Charm Incorporated* (originally called *Bread Upon the Waters*) tells of Jim Targatt, a Wall Street financier who has married 'wardrift' – a refugee from the Russian Revolution – and finds himself expected to help her extended family make their way in the New World. Some of them require accommodation, others money or business introductions – and all of them regular meals in expensive Eastern European restaurants. It is a scenario one would expect to lead to disaster: the good-natured husband bled dry by his crafty in-laws. But Wharton's approach is far more imaginative, as Jim begins to recognise that the charm which characterises the Kouradjines is not a smokescreen, but something of substantial value.

Two of the tales, *Pomegranate Seed* and *The Looking-Glass*, are commonly classified as ghost stories, though only one involves definite dealings with the supernatural. A fascinating aspect of Wharton's writing is the disjunction between her highly sophisticated, ironic prose style and her fondness for plots which rely on old-fashioned devices such as letters and sudden deaths. In *Pomegranate Seed*, letters play a crucial part, arriving mysteriously to torment a lawyer and his new wife. (The title refers to the legend of Proserpine, abducted by Pluto and fatally tempted to eat the fruit of the underworld.) The story's effectiveness lies partly in Wharton's brilliant description of the young wife's conflicting emotions, and partly in the use of two devices which make an alarming situation more frightening still: the buckling of the one person who seems to offer stability and safety, and the insistence that modern life – 'sky-scrapers, advertisements, telephones, wireless, aeroplanes, movies, motors, and all the rest of the twentieth century' – cannot supplant mysterious forces 'as old as the world'.

The collection unsparingly satirises the wealthy class from which Wharton herself came. Jim Targatt starts out indifferent to the lot of the poor: 'as he was always assured of a good meal himself, it never much disturbed him that others were not.' In *The Looking-Glass*, the old masseuse Mrs Attlee pays Mrs Clingsland, her employer, a splendid back-handed compliment: 'There was nothing she wouldn't do for you, if ever for a moment you could get her to stop thinking about herself … and that's saying a good deal, for a rich lady.'

Mrs Attlee is blessed with Irish eloquence (she remembers Mrs Clingsland's bed 'with lace a yard deep on the sheets'), and Wharton's description of it might equally be applied to her own prose: 'a gift for evoking in a few words scenes of half-understood opulence and leisure, like a guide leading a stranger through the gallery of a palace in the twilight, and now and again lifting a lamp to a shimmering Rembrandt or a jewelled Rubens.' Wharton seldom uses similes, which makes them all the more striking when she does; one of the funniest and most ingenious comes in *Duration*, which brings two centenarians into conflict: 'extricating Symington from his armchair was like hooking up a broken cork which, at each prod, slips down farther into the neck of the bottle.'

There is great skill, too, in her use of motifs. The title of *The Looking-Glass* refers not only to the mirror in which Mrs Clingsland sees her beauty fading, but also to the one her masseuse uses to see whether there is breath in a dying man's body. *Permanent Wave*, though the plot is forced, is worth reading for the joyous way in which the heroine – reflecting at the hairdresser on her imminent elopement – measures out her life in perms.

When *The World Over* was published in 1936 (the year before Wharton's death), the *Catholic World* declared that '*Charm Incorporated*, *Confession* and *Roman Fever* belong among the finest short stories she has ever done'. I would go further, and say that *Confession* is one of the most unusual and affecting love stories by any author. Certainly, there are elements of melodrama: a trial for murder; a physical collapse at a crucial moment; a letter which may contain appalling revelations. But these are eclipsed by the expertise with which Wharton unfolds the central mystery (what keeps the ladylike Mrs Carson in thrall to her coarse travelling companion?), and an ending which is not only highly original, but combines dignity and intensity to a rare degree. It may be seen as Wharton's own riposte to *Pomegranate Seed* – and, indeed, to any story you can think of that hinges on a fateful letter.

Like *Pomegranate Seed*, *Roman Fever* needs to be read twice for all its subtleties to be appreciated. The plot is a meandering one: two middle-aged American ladies sit on a terrace overlooking Rome and contemplate their lives, teenage daughters and deceased husbands, gradually realising how little they know each other despite twenty-five years' acquaintance. (One of Wharton's cleverest devices is to present observations apparently to be taken at face value, only to undermine them a moment later: 'So these two ladies visualised each other, each through the wrong end of her little telescope.') You could be forgiven for wondering whether the story is more than an excuse to evoke the magic of Rome at twilight: 'Her gaze turned toward the Colosseum. Already its golden flank was drowned in purple shadow, and above it the sky curved crystal clear, without light or colour. It was the moment when afternoon and evening hang balanced in mid-heaven.' But Wharton, with the skill accrued from half a lifetime as an author, is merely playing with us, and her closing sentence delivers the sort of shock which only the best short-story writers could match: she is like a wasp lazily circling a group of picnickers before imparting an acute, unforgettable sting.

Anthony Gardner

CHARM INCORPORATED*

I

'J im! I'm afraid. . . I'm dreadfully afraid. . .'

James Targatt's wife knelt by his armchair, the dark hair flung off her forehead, her dark eyes large with tears as they yearned up at him through those incredibly long lashes.

'Afraid? Why – what's the matter?' he retorted, annoyed at being disturbed in the slow process of digesting the dinner he had just eaten at Nadeja's last new restaurant – a Ukrainian one this time. For they went to a different restaurant every night, usually, at Nadeja's instigation, hunting out the most exotic that New York at the high tide of its prosperity had to offer. 'That sturgeon stewed in cream –' he thought wearily. 'Well, what is it?'

'It's Boris, darling. I'm afraid Boris is going to marry a film-star. That Halma Hoboe, you know. . . She's the greatest of them all. . .' By this time the tears were running down Nadeja's cheeks. Targatt averted his mind from the sturgeon long enough to wonder if he would ever begin to understand his wife, much less his wife's family.

'Halma Hoboe? Well, why on earth shouldn't he? Has she got her divorce from the last man all right?'

'Yes, of course.' Nadeja was still weeping. 'But I thought perhaps you'd mind Boris's leaving us. He will have to stay out at Hollywood now, he says. And I shall miss my brother

* Originally published under the title: *Bread Upon the Waters.*

so dreadfully. Hollywood's very far from New York – no? We shall all miss Boris, shan't we, James?'

'Yes, yes. Of course. Great boy, Boris! Funny, to be related to a movie-star. 'My sister-in-law, Halma Hoboe'. Well, as long as he couldn't succeed on the screen himself –' said Targatt, suddenly sounding a latent relief, which came to the surface a moment later. *'She'll* have to pay his bills now,' he muttered, too low for his wife to hear. He reached out for a second cigar, let his head sink back comfortably against the chair-cushions, and thought to himself: 'Well, perhaps the luck's turning. . .' For it was the first time, in the eight years of his marriage to Nadeja, that any information imparted to him concerning her family had not immediately led up to his having to draw another cheque.

II

James Targatt had always been on his guard against any form of sentimental weakness; yet now, as he looked back on his life, he began to wonder if the one occasion on which he had been false to this principle might not turn out to be his best stroke of business.

He had not had much difficulty in guarding himself against marriage. He had never felt an abstract yearning for fatherhood, or believed that to marry an old-fashioned affectionate girl, who hated society, and wanted to stay at home and darn and scrub, would really help an ambitious man in his career. He thought it was probably cheaper in the end to have your darning and scrubbing done for you by professionals, even if they came from one of those extortionate valeting establishments that used, before the depression, to charge a dollar a minute for such services. And eventually he found a stranded German widow who came to him on starvation wages, fed him well and inexpensively, and kept the flat looking as fresh and shiny as a racing-yacht.

So there was no earthly obligation for him to marry; and when he suddenly did so, no question of expediency had entered into the arrangement.

He supposed afterward that what had happened to him was what people called falling in love. He had never allowed for that either, and even now he was not sure if it was the right name for the knock-down blow dealt to him by his first sight of Nadeja. Her name told you her part of the story clearly enough. She came straight out of that struggling mass of indistinguishable human misery that Targatt called 'Wardrift'. One day – he still wondered how, for he was always fiercely on his guard against such intrusions – she had forced her way into his office, and tried to sell him (of all things!) a picture painted by her brother Serge. They were all starving, she said; and very likely it was true. But that had not greatly moved him. He had heard the same statement made too often by too many people, and it was too painfully connected in his mind with a dreaded and rapidly increasing form of highway robbery called 'Appeals'. Besides, Targat's imagination was not particularly active, and as he was always sure of a good meal himself, it never much disturbed him to be told that others were not. So he couldn't to this day have told you how it came about that he bought Serge's picture on the spot, and married Nadeja a few weeks afterward. He had been knocked on the head – sandbagged; a regular hold-up. That was the only way to describe it.

Nadeja made no attempt to darn or scrub for him – which was perhaps just as well, as he liked his comforts. On the contrary, she made friends at once with the German widow, and burdened that industrious woman with the additional care of her own wardrobe, which was negligible before her marriage, but increased rapidly after she became Mrs. Targatt. There was a second servant's room above the flat, and Targatt rather reluctantly proposed that they should get in a girl to help Hilda; but Nadeja said, no, she didn't believe Hilda would care for that; and the room would do so nicely for Paul, her younger brother, the one who was studying to be a violinist.

Targatt hated music, and suffered acutely (for a New Yorker) from persistently recurring noises; but Paul, a nice boy, also with long-lashed eyes, moved into the room next to Hilda's, and practised the violin all day and most of the night. The room was directly over that which Targatt now shared with Nadeja – and of which all but the space occupied by his shaving-stand had by this time become her exclusive property. But he bore with Paul's noise, and it was Hilda who struck. She said she loved music that gave her *Heimweh*, but this kind only kept her awake; and to Targatt's horror she announced her intention of leaving at the end of the month.

It was the biggest blow he had ever had since he had once – and once only – been on the wrong side of the market. He had no time to hunt for another servant, and was sure Nadeja would not know how to find one. Nadeja, when he broke the news to her, acquiesced in this view of her incapacity. 'But why do we want a servant? I could never see,' she said. 'And Hilda's room would do very nicely for my sister Olga, who is learning to be a singer. She and Paul could practise together –'

'Oh, Lord,' Targatt interjected.

'And we could all go out to restaurants; a different one every night; it's much more fun, isn't it? And there are people who come in and clean – no? Hilda was a robber – I didn't want to tell you, but . . .'

Within a week the young Olga, whose eyelashes were even longer than Paul's, was settled in the second servant's room, and within a month Targatt had installed a grand piano in his own drawing-room (where it took up all the space left by Nadeja's divan), so that Nadeja could accompany Olga when Paul was not available.

III

Targatt had never, till that moment, thought much about Nadeja's family. He understood that his father-in-law had been a Court dignitary of high standing, with immense landed estates, and armies of slaves – no, he believed they didn't have slaves, or serfs, or whatever they called them, any longer in those outlandish countries east or south of Russia. Targatt was not strong on geography. He did not own an atlas, and had never yet had time to go to the Public Library and look up his father-in-law's native heath. In fact, he had never had time to read, or to think consecutively on any subject but money-making; he knew only that old man Kouradjine had been a big swell in some country in which the Bolsheviks had confiscated everybody's property, and where the women (and the young men too) apparently all had long eyelashes. But that was all part of a vanished fairy-tale; at present the old man was only Number So-much on one Near East Relief list, while Paul and Olga and the rest of them (Targatt wasn't sure even yet how many there were) figured on similar lists, though on a more modest scale, since they were supposedly capable of earning their own living. But were they capable of it, and was there any living for them to earn? That was what Targatt in the course of time began to ask himself.

Targatt was not a particularly sociable man; but in his bachelor days he had fancied inviting a friend to dine now and then, chiefly to have the shine on his mahogany table marvelled at, and Hilda's *Wiener-schnitzel* praised. This was all over now. His meals were all taken in restaurants – a different one each time; and they were usually shared with Paul, Olga, Serge (the painter) and the divorced sister, Katinka, who had three children and a refugee lover, Dmitri.

At first this state of affairs was very uncomfortable, and even painful, for Targatt; but since it seemed inevitable he adjusted himself to it, and buried his private cares in an increased business activity.

His activity was, in fact, tripled by the fact that it was no longer restricted to his own personal affairs, but came more and more to include such efforts as organizing an exhibition of Serge's pictures, finding the funds for Paul's violin tuition, trying to make it worth somebody's while to engage Olga for a concert tour, pushing Katinka into a saleswoman's job at a fashionable dress-maker's, and persuading a friend in a bank to recommend Dmitri as interpreter to foreign clients. All this was difficult enough, and if Targatt had not been sustained by Nadeja's dogged optimism his courage might have failed him; but the crowning problem was how to deal with the youngest brother, Boris, who was just seventeen, and had the longest eyelashes of all. Boris was too old to be sent to school, too young to be put into a banker's or broker's office, and too smilingly irresponsible to hold the job for twenty-four hours if it had been offered to him. Targatt, for three years after his marriage, had had only the vaguest idea of Boris's existence, for he was not among the first American consignment of the family. But suddenly he drifted in alone, from Odessa or Athens, and joined the rest of the party at the restaurant. By this time the Near East Relief Funds were mostly being wound up, and in spite of all Targatt's efforts it was impossible to get financial aid for Boris, so for the first months he just lolled in a pleasant aimless way on Nadeja's divan; and as he was very particular about the quality of his cigarettes, and consumed a large supply daily, Targatt for the first time began to regard one of Nadeja's family with a certain faint hostility.

Boris might have been less of a trial if, by the time he came, Targatt had been able to get the rest of the family on their legs; but, however often he repeated this attempt, they invariably toppled over on him. Serge could not sell his pictures, Paul could not get an engagement in an orchestra, Olga had given up singing for dancing, so that her tuition had to begin all over again; and to think of Dmitri and Katinka, and Katinka's three children, was not conducive to repose at the end of a hard day in Wall Street.

Yet in spite of everything Targatt had never really been able to remain angry for more than a few moments with any member of the Kouradjine group. For some years this did not particularly strike him; he was given neither to self-analysis nor to the dissection of others, except where business dealings were involved. He had been taught, almost in the nursery, to discern, and deal with, the motives determining a given course in business; but he knew no more of human nature's other mainsprings than if the nursery were still his habitat. He was vaguely conscious that Nadeja was aware of this, and that it caused her a faint amusement. Once, when they had been dining with one of his business friends, and the latter's wife, an ogling bore, had led the talk to the shop-worn question of how far mothers ought to enlighten their little girls on – well, you know. . . Just *how much* ought they to be taught? That was the delicate point, Mrs. Targatt, wasn't it? – Nadeja, thus cornered, had met the question with a gaze of genuine bewilderment. 'Taught? Do they have to be *taught*? I think it is Nature who will tell them – no? But myself I should first teach dressmaking and cooking,' she said with her shadowy smile. And now, reviewing the Kouradjine case, Targatt suddenly thought: 'But that's it! Nature *does* teach the Kouradjines. It's a gift like a tenor voice. The thing is to know how to make the best use of it –' and he fell to musing on this newly discovered attribute. It was – what? Charm? Heaven forbid! The very word made his flesh creep with memories of weary picnics and wearier dinners where, with pink food in fluted papers, the discussion of 'What is Charm?' had formed the staple diet. 'I'd run a mile from a woman with charm; and so would most men,' Targatt thought with a retrospective shudder.

And he tried, for the first time, to make a conscious inventory of Nadeja's attributes.

She was not beautiful; he was certain of that. He was not good at seeing people, really seeing them, even when they were before his eyes, much less at visualizing them in absence. When Nadeja was away all he could ever evoke of her was a pleasant blur. But he wasn't such a blind bat as not to know when a woman was beautiful. Beauty, however, was made to look at, not to live with; he had never wanted to marry a beautiful woman. And Nadeja wasn't clever, either; not in talk, that is. (And that, he mused, was certainly one of her qualities.) With regard to the other social gifts, so-called: cards, for instance? Well, he knew she and Katinka were not above fishing out an old pack and telling their fortunes, when they thought he wasn't noticing; but anything as scientific as bridge frightened her, and she had the good sense not to try to learn. So much for society; and as for the home – well, she could hardly be called a good housekeeper, he supposed. But remembering his mother, who had been accounted a paragon in that line, he gave thanks for this deficiency of Nadeja's also. Finally he said to himself: 'I seem to like her for all the things she is *not*.' This was not satisfactory; but he could do no better. 'Well, somehow, she fits into the cracks,' he concluded; and inadequate as this also sounded, he felt it might turn out to be a clue to the Kouradjines. Yes, they certainly fitted in; squeezing you a little, overlapping you a good deal, but never – and there was the point – sticking into you like the proverbial thorn, or crowding you uncomfortably, or for any reason making you wish they weren't there.

This fact, of which he had been dimly conscious from the first, arrested his attention now because he had a sudden glimpse of its business possibilities. Little Boris had only had to borrow a hundred dollars of him for the trip to Hollywood, and behold little Boris was already affianced to the world's leading movie-star! In the light of this surprising event Targatt suddenly recalled that Katinka, not long before, had asked him if he wouldn't give Dmitri, who had not been a success at the bank, a letter recommending him for some sort of employment in the office of a widowed millionaire who was the highest light on Targatt's business horizon. Targatt had received the suggestion without enthusiasm. 'Your sister's crazy,' he said to Nadeja. 'How can I recommend that fellow to a man like Bellamy? Has he ever had any business training?'

'Well, we know Mr. Bellamy's looking for a book-keeper, because he asked you if you knew of one,' said Nadeja.

'Yes; but what are Dmitri's qualifications? Does he know anything whatever about book-keeping?'

'No; not yet. But he says perhaps he could buy a little book about it.'

'Oh, Lord –' Targatt groaned.

'Even so, you don't think you could recommend him, darling?'

'No; I couldn't, I'm afraid.'

Nadeja did not insist; she never insisted. 'I've found out a new restaurant, where they make much better blinys. Shall I tell them all to meet us there tonight at half-past eight?' she suggested.

Now, in the light of Boris's news, Targatt began to think this conversation over. Dmitri was an irredeemable fool; but Katinka – what about giving the letter for old Bellamy to Katinka? Targatt didn't see exactly how he could word it; but he had an idea that Nadeja would tell him. Those were the ways in which she was really clever. A few days later he asked: 'Has Dmitri got a job yet?'

She looked at him in surprise. 'No; as you couldn't recommend him he didn't buy the book.'

'Oh, damn the book. . . See here, Nadeja; supposing I were to give Katinka a letter for old Bellamy?'

He had made the suggestion with some embarrassment, half expecting that he would have to explain. But not to Nadeja.

'Oh, darling, you always think of the right thing,' she answered, kissing him; and as he had foreseen she told him just how to word the letter.

'And I will lend her my silver fox to wear,' she added. Certainly the social education of the Kouradjines had been far more comprehensive than Targatt's.

Katinka went to see Mr. Bellamy, and when she returned she reported favourably on the visit. Nothing was as yet decided about Dmitri, as she had been obliged to confess that he had had no training as an accountant; but Mr. Bellamy had been very kind, and had invited her to come to his house some afternoon to see his pictures.

From this visit also Katinka came back well-pleased, though she seemed not to have accomplished anything further with regard to Dmitri. She had, however, been invited by Mr. Bellamy to dine and go to a play; and a few weeks afterward she said to Targatt and Nadeja: 'I think I will live with Mr. Bellamy. He has an empty flat that I could have, and he would furnish it beautifully.'

Though Targatt prided himself on an unprejudiced mind he winced slightly at this suggestion. It seemed cruel to Dmitri, and decidedly uncomfortable as far as Targatt and Nadeja were concerned.

'But, Katinka, if Bellamy's so gone on you, he ought to marry you,' he said severely.

Katinka nodded her assent. 'Certainly he ought. And I think he will, after I have lived with him a few months.'

This upset every single theory of Targatt's with regard to his own sex. 'But, my poor girl – if you go and live with a man first like . . . like any woman he could have for money, why on earth should he want to marry you afterward?'

Katinka looked at him calmly. Her eyelashes were not as long as Nadeja's, but her eyes were as full of wisdom. 'Habit,' she said simply; and in an instant Targat's conventional world was in fragments at his feet. Who knew better than he did that if you once had the Kouradjine habit you couldn't be cured of it? He said nothing more, and sat back to watch what happened to Mr. Bellamy.

IV

Mr. Bellamy did not offer Dmitri a position as book-keeper; but soon after his marriage to Katinka he took him into his house as social secretary. Targatt had a first movement of surprise and disapproval, but he saw that Nadeja did not share it. 'That's very nice,' she said. 'I was sure Katinka would not desert Dmitri. And Mr. Bellamy is so generous. He is going to adopt Katinka's three children.'

But it must not be thought that the fortunes of all the Kouradjines ran as smoothly. For a brief moment Targatt had imagined that the infatuated Bellamy was going to assume the charge of the whole tribe; but Wall Street was beginning to be uneasy, and Mr. Bellamy restricted his hospitality to Katinka's children and Dmitri, and, like many of the very rich, manifested no interest in those whose misfortunes did not immediately interfere with his own comfort. Thus vanished even the dream of a shared responsibility, and Targatt saw himself facing a business outlook decidedly less dazzling, and with a still considerable number of Kouradjines to provide for. Olga, in particular, was a cause of some anxiety. She was less adaptable, less suited to fitting into cracks, than the others, and her various experiments in song and dance had all broken down for lack of perseverance. But she was (at least so Nadeja thought) by far the best-looking of the family; and finally Targatt decided to pay for her journey to Hollywood, in the hope that Boris would put her in the way of becoming a screen star. This suggestion, however, was met by a telegram from Boris ominously dated from Reno: 'Don't send Olga am divorcing Halma.'

For the first time since his marriage Targatt felt really discouraged. Were there perhaps too many Kouradjines, and might the Kouradjine habit after all be beginning to wear thin? The family were all greatly perturbed by Boris's news, and when – after the brief interval required to institute and complete divorce proceedings against his film star – Boris left Reno and turned up in New York, his air of unperturbed good-humour was felt to be unsuitable to the occasion. Nadeja, always hopeful, interpreted it as meaning that he was going to marry another and even richer star; but Boris said God forbid, and no more Hollywood for him. Katinka and Bellamy did not invite him to come and stay, and the upshot of it was that his bed was made up on the Targatts' drawing-room divan, while he shared the bathroom with Targatt and Nadeja.

Things dragged on in this way for some weeks, till one day Nadeja came privately to her husband. 'He has got three millions,' she whispered with wide eyes. 'Only yesterday was he sure. The cheque has come. Do you think, darling, she ought to have allowed him more?'

Targatt did not think so; he was inarticulate over Boris's achievement. 'What's he going to do with it?' he gasped.

'Well, I think first he will invest it, and then he will go to the Lido. There is a young girl there, I believe, that he is in love with. I knew Boris would not divorce for nothing. He is going there to meet her.'

Targatt could not disguise an impulse of indignation. Before investing his millions, was Boris not going to do anything for his family? Nadeja said she had thought of that too; but Boris said he had invested the money that morning, and of course there would be no interest coming in till the next quarter. And meanwhile he was so much in love that he had taken his passage for the following day on the *Berengaria*. Targatt thought that only natural, didn't he?

Targatt swallowed his ire, and said, yes, he supposed it was natural enough. After all, if the boy had found a young girl he could really love and respect, and if he had the money to marry her and settle down, no one could blame him for rushing off to press his suit. And Boris rushed.

But meanwhile the elimination of two Kouradjines had not had the hoped-for effect of reducing the total number of the tribe. On the contrary, that total had risen; for suddenly three new members had appeared. One was an elderly and completely ruined Princess (a distant cousin, Nadeja explained) with whom old Kouradjine had decided to contract a tardy alliance, now that the rest of the family were provided for. ('He could do no less,' Katinka and Nadeja mysteriously agreed.) And the other, and more sensational, newcomers were two beautiful young creatures, known respectively to the tribe as Nick and Mouna, but whose difficulties at the passport office made it seem that there were legal doubts as to their remaining names. These difficulties, through Targatt's efforts, were finally overcome, and snatched from the jaws of Ellis Island, Nick and Mouna joyfully joined the party at another new restaurant, 'The Transcaucasian', which Nadeja had recently discovered.

Targatt's immensely enlarged experience of human affairs left him in little doubt as to the parentage of Nick and Mouna, and when Nadeja whispered to him one night (through the tumult of Boris's late bath next door): 'You see, poor Papa felt he could not longer fail to provide for them,' Targatt did not dream of asking why.

But he now had no less than seven Kouradjines more or less dependent on him, and the next night he sat up late and did some figuring and thinking. Even to Nadeja he could not explain in blunt language the result of this vigil; but he said to her the following day: 'What's become of that flat of Bellamy's that Katinka lived in before –'

'Why, he gave the lease to Katinka as a wedding-present; but it seems that people are no more as rich as they were, and as it's such a very handsome flat, and the rent is high, the tenants can no longer afford to keep it –'

'Well,' said Targatt with sudden resolution, 'tell your sister if she'll make a twenty-five per cent cut on the rent I'll take over the balance of the lease.'

Nadeja gasped. 'Oh, James, you are an angel! But what do you think you could then do with it?'

Targatt threw back his shoulders. 'Live in it,' he recklessly declared.

V

It was the first time (except when he had married Nadeja) that he had ever been reckless; and there was no denying that he enjoyed the sensation. But he had not acted wholly for the sake of enjoyment; he had an ulterior idea. What that idea was he did not choose to communicate to any one at present. He merely asked Katinka, who, under the tuition of Mr. Bellamy's experienced butler, had developed some rudimentary ideas of house-keeping, to provide Nadeja with proper servants, and try to teach her how to use them; and he then announced to Nadeja that he had made up his mind to do a little entertaining. He and Nadeja had already made a few fashionable acquaintances at the Bellamys', and these they proceeded to invite to the new flat, and to feed with exotic food, and stimulate with abstruse cocktails. At these dinners Targatt's new friends met the younger and lovelier of the Kouradjines: Paul, Olga, Nick and Mouna, and they always went away charmed with the encounter.

Considerable expense was involved by this new way of life; and still more when Nadeja, at Targatt's instigation, invited Olga, Nick and Mouna to come and live with them. Nadeja was overcome with gratitude at this suggestion; but her gratitude, like all her other emotions, was so exquisitely modulated that it fell on Targatt like the gentle dew from heaven, merely fostering in him a new growth of tenderness. But still Targatt did not explain himself. He had his idea, and knowing that Nadeja would not bother him with questions he sat back quietly and waited, though Wall Street was growing more and more unsettled, and there had been no further news of Boris, and Paul and Olga were still without a job.

The Targatts' little dinners, and Nadeja's exclusive cocktail parties, began to be the rage in a set far above the Bellamys'. There were almost always one or two charming young Kouradjines present; but they were now so sought after in smartest Park Avenue and gayest Long Island that Targatt and Nadeja had to make sure of securing their presence beforehand, so there was never any danger of there being too many on the floor at once.

On the contrary, there were occasions when they all simultaneously failed to appear; and on one of these evenings, Targatt, conscious that the party had not 'come off', was about to vent his irritation against the absent Serge, when Nadeja said gently: 'I'm sorry Serge didn't tell you. But I think he was married today to Mrs. Leeper.'

'Mrs. Leeper? Not the Dazzle Tooth-Paste woman he met at the Bellamys', who wanted him to decorate her ball-room?'

'Yes; but I think she did not after all want him to decorate her ball-room. And so she has married him instead.'

A year earlier Targatt would have had no word but an uncomprehending groan. But since then his education had proceeded by leaps and bounds, and now he simply said: 'I see –' and turned back to his breakfast with a secret smile. He had received Serge's tailor's bill the day before, and had been rehearsing half the night what he was going to say to Serge when they met. But now he merely remarked: 'That woman has a two million dollar income,' and thought to himself that the experiment with the flat was turning out better than he could have imagined. If Serge could be disposed of so easily there was no cause to despair of Paul or Olga. 'Hasn't Mrs. Leeper a nephew?' he asked Nadeja; who, as if she had read his thought, replied regretfully: 'Yes; but I'm afraid he's married.'

'Oh, well – send Boris to talk to him!' Targatt jeered; and Nadeja, who never laughed, smiled a little and replied: 'Boris too will soon be married.' She handed her husband the morning papers, which he had not yet had time to examine, and he read, in glowing headlines, the announcement of the marriage in London of Prince Boris Kouradjine, son of Prince Peter Kouradjine, hereditary sovereign of Daghestan, and Chamberlain at the court of his late Imperial Majesty the Czar Nicholas, to Miss Mamie Guggins of Rapid Rise, Oklahoma. 'Boris has a little exaggerated our father's rank,' Nadeja commented; but Targatt said thoughtfully: 'No one can exaggerate the Guggins fortune.' And Nadeja gave a quiet sigh.

It must not be supposed that this rise in the fortunes of the Kouradjines was of any direct benefit to Targatt. He had never expected that, or even hoped it. No Kouradjine had ever suggested making any return for the sums expended by Targatt in vainly educating and profitably dressing his irresistible in-laws; nor had Targatt's staggering restaurant bills been reduced by any offer of participation. Only the old Princess (as it was convenient, with so many young ones about, to call her when she was out of hearing) had said tearfully, on her wedding-day: 'Believe me, my good James, what you have done for us all will not be forgotten when we return to Daghestan.' And she spoke with such genuine emotion, the tears were so softening to her tired magnificent eyes, that Targatt, at the moment, felt himself repaid.

Other and more substantial returns he did draw from his alliance with the Kouradjines; and it was the prospect of these which had governed his conduct. From the day when it had occurred to him to send Katinka to intercede with Mr. Bellamy,

Targatt had never once swerved from his purpose. And slowly but surely he was beginning to reap his reward.

Mr. Bellamy, for instance, had not seen his way to providing for the younger Kouradjines; but he was ready enough to let Targatt in on the ground floor of one of those lucrative deals usually reserved for the already wealthy. Mrs. Leeper, in her turn, gave him the chance to buy a big block of Dazzle Tooth-Paste shares on exceptional terms; and as fashion and finance became aware of the younger Kouradjines, and fell under their spell, Targatt's opportunities for making quick turnovers became almost limitless. And now a pleasant glow stole down his spine at the thought that all previous Kouradjine alliances paled before the staggering wealth of Boris's bride. 'Boris really does owe me a good turn,' he mused; but he had no expectation that it would be done with Boris's knowledge. The new Princess Boris was indeed induced to hand over her discarded wardrobe to Olga and Mouna, and Boris presented cigarette cases to his brothers and brother-in-law; but here his prodigalities ended. Targatt, however, was not troubled; for years he had longed to meet the great Mr. Guggins, and here he was, actually related to that gentleman's only child!

Mr. Guggins, when under the influence of domestic happiness or alcohol, was almost as emotional as the Kouradjines. On his return to New York, after the parting from his only child, he was met on the dock by Targatt and Nadeja, who suggested his coming to dine that night at a jolly new restaurant with all the other Kouradjines; and Mrs. Guggins was so much drawn to the old Princess, to whom she confided how difficult it was to get reliable window-washers at Rapid Rise, that the next day Targatt, as he would have put it, had the old man in his pocket. Mr. Guggins stayed a week in New York, and when he departed Targatt knew enough about the Guggins industries to make some very useful reinvestments; and Mrs. Guggins carried off Olga as her social secretary.

VI

Stimulated by these successive achievements Targat's tardily developed imagination was growing like an Indian juggler's tree. He no longer saw any limits to what might be done with the Kouradjines. He had already found a post for the old Prince as New York representative of a leading firm of Paris picture-dealers, Paul and Nick were professional dancers at fashionable night-clubs, and for the moment only Mouna, the lovely but difficult, remained on Targat's mind and his pay-roll.

It was the first time in his life that Targatt had tasted the fruits of ease, and he found them surprisingly palatable. He was no longer young, it took him more time than of old to get around a golf-course, and he occasionally caught himself telling his good stories twice over to the same listener. But life was at once exciting and peaceful, and he had to own that his interests had been immensely enlarged. All that, of course, he owed in the first instance to Nadeja. Poor Nadeja – she was not as young as she had been, either. She was still slender and supple, but there were little lines in the corners of her eyes, and a certain droop of the mouth. Others might not notice these symptoms, Targatt thought; but they had not escaped *him*. For Targatt, once so unseeing in the presence of beauty, had now become an adept in appraising human flesh-and-blood, and smiled knowingly when his new friends commended Mouna's young charms, or inclined the balance in favour of the more finished Olga. There was nothing any one could tell him now about the relative 'values' of the Kouradjines: he had them tabulated as if they were vintage wines, and it was a comfort to him to reflect that Nadeja was, after all, the one whose market value was least considerable. It was sheer luck – a part of his miraculous Kouradjine luck – that his choice had fallen on the one Kouradjine about whom there was never likely to be the least fuss or scandal; and after an exciting day in Wall Street, or a fatiguing struggle to extricate Paul or Mouna from some fresh scrape, he would sink back with satisfaction into his own unruffled domesticity.

There came a day, however, when he began to feel that the contrast between his wife and her sisters was too much to Nadeja's disadvantage. Was it because the others had smarter clothes – or, like Katinka, finer jewels? Poor Nadeja, he reflected, had never had any jewels since her engagement ring; and that was a shabby affair. Was it possible, Targatt conjectured, that as middle age approached she was growing dowdy, and needed the adventitious enhancements of dress-maker and beauty doctor? Half sheepishly he suggested that she oughtn't to let herself be outdone by Katinka, who was two or three years her senior; and he reinforced the suggestion by a diamond chain from Cartier's and a good-humoured hint that she might try Mrs. Bellamy's dress-maker.

Nadeja received the jewel with due raptures, and appeared at their next dinner in a gown which was favourably noticed by every one present. Katinka said: 'Well, at last poor Nadeja is really *dressed*,' and Mouna sulked visibly, and remarked to her brother-in-law: 'If you want the right people to ask me about you might let me get a few clothes at Nadeja's place.'

All this was as it should be, and Targat's satisfaction increased as he watched his wife's returning bloom. It seemed funny to him that, even on a sensible woman like Nadeja, clothes and jewels should act as a tonic; but then the Kouradjines *were* funny, and heaven knew Targatt had no reason to begrudge them any of their little fancies – especially now that Olga's engagement to Mrs. Guggins' brother (representative of the Guggins interests in London and Paris) had been officially announced. When the news came, Targatt gave his wife a pair of emerald earrings, and suggested that they should take their summer holiday in Paris.

It was the same winter that New York was thrown into a flutter by the announcement that the famous portrait painter,

Axel Svengaart, was coming over to 'do' a chosen half-dozen sitters. Svengaart had never been to New York before, had always sworn that anybody who wanted to be painted by him must come to his studio at Oslo; but it suddenly struck him that the American background might give a fresh quality to his work, and after painting one lady getting out of her car in front of her husband's motor-works, and Mrs. Guggins against the background of a spouting oil-well at Rapid Rise, he appeared in New York to organise a show of these sensational canvases. New York was ringing with the originality and audacity of this new experiment. After expecting to be 'done' in the traditional setting of the Gothic library or the Quattro Cento *salon*, it was incredibly exciting to be portrayed literally surrounded by the acknowledged sources of one's wealth; and the wife of a fabulously rich plumber was nearly persuaded to be done stepping out of her bath, in a luxury bathroom fitted with the latest ablutionary appliances.

Fresh from these achievements, Axel Svengaart carried his Viking head and Parisian monocle from one New York drawing-room to another, gazing, appraising – even, though rarely, praising – but absolutely refusing to take another order, or to postpone by a single day the date of his sailing. 'I've got it all here,' he said, touching first his brow and then his pocket; and the dealer who acted as his impresario let it be understood that even the most exaggerated offers would be rejected.

Targatt had, of course, met the great man. In old days he would have been uncomfortably awed by the encounter; but now he could joke easily about the Gugginses, and even ask Svengaart if he had not been struck by his sister-in-law, who was Mrs. Guggins's social secretary, and was about to marry Mr. Guggins's Paris representative.

'Ah – the lovely Kouradjine; yes. She made us some delicious blinys,' Svengaart nodded approvingly; but Targatt saw with surprise that as a painter he was uninterested in Olga's plastic possibilities.

'Ah, well, I suppose you've had enough of us – I hear you're off this week.'

The painter dropped his monocle. 'Yes, I've had enough.' It was after dinner, at the Bellamys', and abruptly he seated himself on the sofa at Targatt's side. 'I don't like your frozen food,' he pursued. 'There's only one thing that would make me put off my sailing.' He readjusted his monocle and looked straight at Targatt. 'If you'll give me the chance to paint Mrs. Targatt – oh, for that I'd wait another month.'

Targatt stared at him, too surprised to answer. Nadeja – the great man wanted to paint Nadeja! The idea aroused so many conflicting considerations that his reply, when it came, was a stammer. 'Why, really . . . this is a surprise . . . a great honour, of course. . .' A vision of Svengaar's price for a mere head thrust itself hideously before his eyes. Svengaart, seeing him as it were encircled by millionaires, probably took him for a very rich man – was perhaps manoeuvring to extract an extra big offer from him. For what other inducement could there be to paint Nadeja? Targatt turned the question with a joke. 'I suspect you're confusing me with my brother-in-law Bellamy. He ought to have persuaded you to paint his wife. But I'm afraid my means wouldn't allow . . .'

The other interrupted him with an irritated gesture. 'Please – my dear sir. I can never be 'persuaded' to do a portrait. And in the case of Mrs. Targatt I had no idea of selling you her picture. If I paint her, it would be for myself.'

Targatt's stare widened. 'For yourself? You mean – you'd paint the picture just to keep it?' He gave an embarrassed laugh. 'Nadeja would be enormously flattered, of course. But, between ourselves, would you mind telling me why you want to do her?'

Svengaart stood up with a faint laugh. 'Because she's the only really paintable woman I've seen here. The lines are incomparable for a full-length. And I can't tell you how I should enjoy the change.'

Targatt continued to stare. Murmurs of appreciation issued from his parched lips. He remembered now that Svengaart's charge for a three-quarter-length was fifteen thousand dollars. And he wanted to do Nadeja full length for nothing! Only – Targatt reminded himself – the brute wanted to keep the picture. So where was the good? It would only make Nadeja needlessly conspicuous; and to give all those sittings for nothing. . . Well, it looked like sharp practice, somehow. . .

'Of course, as I say, my wife would be immensely flattered; only she's very busy – her family, social obligations and so on; I really can't say. . .'

Svengaart smiled. 'In the course of a portrait I usually make a good many studies; some almost as finished as the final picture. If Mrs. Targatt cared to accept one –'

Targatt flushed to the roots of his thinning hair. A Svengaart study over the drawing-room mantel-piece! ('Yes – nice thing of Nadeja, isn't it? You'd know a Svengaart anywhere. . . It was his own idea; he insisted on doing her. . .')

Nadeja was just lifting a pile of music from the top of the grand piano. She was going to accompany Mouna, who had taken to singing. As she stood with lifted arms, profiled against the faint hues of the tapestried wall, the painter exclaimed: 'There – there! I have it! Don't you see now why I want to do her?'

But Targatt, for the moment, could not speak. Secretly he thought Nadeja looked much as usual – only perhaps a little more tired; she had complained of a headache that morning. But his courage rose to the occasion. 'Ah, my wife's famous 'lines', eh? Well, well, I can't promise – you'd better come over and try to persuade her yourself.'

He was so dizzy with it that as he led Svengaart toward the piano the Bellamys' parquet floor felt like glass under his unsteady feet.

VII

Targatt's rapture was acute but short-lived. Nadeja 'done' by Axel Svengaart – he had measured the extent of it in a flash. He had stood aside and watched her with a deep smile of satisfaction while the light of wonder rose in her eyes; when she turned them on him for approval he had nodded his assent. Of course she must sit to the great man, his glance signalled back. He saw that Svengaart was amused at her having to ask her husband's permission; but this only intensified Targat's satisfaction. They'd see, damn it, if his wife could be ordered about like a professional model! Perhaps the best moment was when, the next day, she said timidly: 'But, Jim, have you thought about the price?' and he answered, his hands in his pockets, an easy smile on his lips: 'There's no price to think about. He's doing you for the sake of your beautiful 'lines'. And we're to have a replica, free gratis. Did you know you had beautiful lines, old Nad?'

She looked at him gravely for a moment. 'I hadn't thought about them for a long time,' she said.

Targatt laughed and tapped her on the shoulder. What a child she was! But afterward it struck him that she had not been particularly surprised by the painter's request. Perhaps she had always known she was paintable, as Svengaart called it. Perhaps – and here he felt a little chill run over him – perhaps Svengaart had spoken to her already, had come to an understanding with her before making his request to Targatt. The idea made Targatt surprisingly uncomfortable, and he reflected that it was the first occasion in their married life when he had suspected Nadeja of even the most innocent duplicity. And this, if it were true, could hardly be regarded as wholly innocent. . .

Targatt shook the thought off impatiently. He was behaving like the fellow in 'Pagliacci'. Really this associating with foreigners might end in turning a plain business man into an opera-singer! It was the day of the first sitting, and as he started for his office he called back gaily to Nadeja: 'Well, so long! And don't let that fellow turn your head.'

He could not get much out of Nadeja about the sittings. It was not that she seemed secretive; but she was never very good at reporting small talk, and things that happened outside of the family circle, even if they happened to herself, always seemed of secondary interest to her. And meanwhile the sittings went on and on. In spite of his free style Svengaart was a slow worker; and he seemed to find Nadeja a difficult subject. Targatt began to brood over the situation: some people thought the fellow handsome, in the lean grey-hound style; and he had an easy cosmopolitan way – the European manner. It was what Nadeja was used to; would she suddenly feel that she had missed something during all these years? Targatt turned cold at the thought. It had never before occurred to him what a humdrum figure he was. The contemplation of his face in the shaving-glass became so distasteful to him that he averted his eyes, and nearly cut his throat in consequence. Nothing of the grey-hound style about him – or the Viking either.

Slowly, as these thoughts revolved in his mind, he began to feel that he, who had had everything from Nadeja, had given her little or nothing in return. What he had done for her people weighed as nothing in this revaluation of their past. The point was: what sort of a life had he given Nadeja? And the answer: No life at all! She had spent her best years looking after other people; he could not remember that she had ever asserted a claim or resented an oversight. And yet she was neither dull nor insipid: she was simply Nadeja – a creature endlessly tolerant, totally unprejudiced, sublimely generous and unselfish.

Well – it would be funny, Targatt thought, with a twist of almost physical pain, if nobody else had been struck by such unusual qualities. If it had taken him over ten years to find them out, others might have been less blind. He had never noticed her 'lines', for instance; yet that painter fellow, the moment he'd clapped eyes on her –!

Targatt sat in his study, twisting about restlessly in his chair. Where *was* Nadeja, he wondered? The winter dusk had fallen, and painters do not work without daylight. The day's sitting must be over – and yet she had not come back. Usually she was always there to greet him on his return from the office. She had taught him to enjoy his afternoon tea, with a tiny caviar sandwich and a slice of lemon, and the samovar was already murmuring by the fire. When she went to see any of her family she always called up to say if she would be late; but the maid said there had been no message from her.

Targatt got up and walked the floor impatiently; then he sat down again, lit a cigarette, and threw it away. Nadeja, he remembered, had not been in the least shocked when Katinka had decided to live with Mr. Bellamy; she had merely wondered if the step were expedient, and had finally agreed with Katinka that it was. Nor had Boris's matrimonial manoeuvres seemed to offend her. She was entirely destitute of moral indignation; this painful reality was now borne in on Targatt for the first time. Cruelty shocked her; but otherwise she seemed to think that people should do as they pleased. Yet, all the while, had she ever done what *she* pleased? There was the torturing enigma! She seemed to allow such latitude to others, yet to ask so little for herself.

Well, but didn't the psychologist fellows say that there was an hour in every woman's life – every self-sacrificing woman's – when the claims of her suppressed self suddenly asserted themselves, body and soul, and she forgot everything else, all her duties, ties, responsibilities? Targatt broke off with a bitter laugh. What did 'duties, ties, responsibilities' mean to Nadeja? No more than to any of the other Kouradjines. Their vocabulary had no parallels with his. He felt a sudden overwhelming loneliness, as if all these years he had been married to a changeling, an opalescent creature swimming up out of the sea. . .

No, she couldn't be at the studio any longer; or if she were, it wasn't to sit for her portrait. Curse the portrait, he thought – why had he ever consented to her sitting to Svengaart? Sheer cupidity; the snobbish ambition to own a Svengaart, the glee of getting one for nothing. The more he proceeded with this self-investigation the less he cared for the figure he cut. But however poor a part he had played so far, he wasn't going to add to it the rôle of the duped husband...

'Damn it, I'll go round there myself and see,' he muttered, squaring his shoulders, and walking resolutely across the room to the door. But as he reached the entrance-hall the faint click of a latchkey greeted him; and sweeter music he had never heard. Nadeja stood in the doorway, pale but smiling. 'Jim – you were not going out again?'

He gave a sheepish laugh. 'Do you know what time it is? I was getting scared.'

'Scared for me?' She smiled again. 'Dear me, yes! It's nearly dinner-time, isn't it?'

He followed her into the drawing-room and shut the door. He felt like a husband in an old-fashioned problem play; and in a moment he had spoken like one. 'Nad, where've you come from?' he broke out abruptly.

'Why, the studio. It was my last sitting.'

'People don't sit for their portraits in the dark.'

He saw a faint surprise in her eyes as she bent to the samovar. 'No; I was not sitting all the time. Not for the last hour or more, I suppose.'

She spoke as quietly as usual, yet he thought he caught a tremor of resentment in her voice. Against himself – or against the painter? But how he was letting his imagination run away with him! He sat down in his accustomed armchair, took the cup of tea she held out. He was determined to behave like a reasonable being, yet never had reason appeared to him so unrelated to reality. 'Ah, well – I suppose you two had a lot of things to talk about. You rather fancy Svengaart, don't you?'

'Oh, yes; I like him very much. Do you know,' she asked earnestly, 'how much he has made during his visit to America? It was of course in confidence that he told me. Two hundred thousand dollars. And he was rich before.'

She spoke so solemnly that Targatt burst into a vague laugh. 'Well, what of it? I don't know that it showed much taste to brag to you about the way he skins his sitters. But it shows he didn't make much of a sacrifice in painting you for nothing,' he said irritably.

'No; I said to him he might have done you too.'

'*Me?*' Targatt's laugh redoubled. 'Well, what did he say to that?'

'Oh, he laughed as you are now laughing,' Nadeja rejoined. 'But he says he will never marry – never.'

Targatt put down his cup with a rattle. '*Never marry?* What the devil are you talking about? Who cares whether he marries, anyhow?' he gasped with a dry throat.

'I do,' said Nadeja.

There was a silence. Nadeja was lifting her teacup to her lips, and something in the calm free movement reminded him of Svengaart's outburst when he had seen her lift the pile of music. For the first time in his life Targatt seemed to himself to be looking at her; and he wondered if it would also be the last. He cleared his throat and tried to speak, to say something immense, magnanimous. 'Well, if –'

'No; it's useless. He will hear nothing. I said to him: "You will never anywhere find such a *plastik* as Mouna's" . . .'

'*Mouna's?*'

She turned to him with a slight shrug. 'Oh, my poor Jim, are you quite blind? Haven't you seen how we have all been trying to make him want to marry Mouna? It will be almost my first failure, I think,' she concluded with a half-apologetic sigh.

Targatt rested his chin on his hands and looked up at her. She looked tired, certainly, and older; too tired and old for any one still well under forty. And Mouna – why in God's name should she be persecuting this man to marry Mouna? It was indecent, it was shocking, it was unbelievable. . . Yet not for a moment did he doubt the truth of what she said.

'Mouna?' he could only repeat stupidly.

'Well, you see, darling, we're all a little anxious about Mouna. And I was so glad when Svengaart asked to paint me, because I thought: "Now's my opportunity." But no, it was not to be.'

Targatt drew a deep breath. He seemed to be inhaling some life-giving element, and it was with the most superficial severity that he said: 'I don't fancy this idea of your throwing your sister at men's heads.'

'No, it was no use,' Nadeja sighed, with her usual complete unawareness of any moral rebuke in his comment.

Targatt stood up uneasily. 'He wouldn't have her at any price?'

She shook her head sadly. 'Foolish man!'

Targatt went up to her and took her abruptly by the wrist. 'Look at me, Nadeja – straight. Did he refuse her because he wanted *you?*'

She gave her light lift of the shoulders, and the rare colour flitted across her pale cheeks. 'Isn't it always the way of men? What they can't get –'

'Ah; so he's been making love to you all this time, has he?'

'But of course not, James. What he wished was to marry me. That is something quite different, is it not?'

'Yes. I see.'

Targatt had released her wrist and turned away. He walked once or twice up and down the length of the room, no more knowing where he was than a man dropped blindfold onto a new planet. He knew what he wanted to do and to say; the words he had made up his mind to speak stood out in letters of fire against the choking blackness. 'You must feel yourself free –' Five words, and so easy to speak! 'Perfectly free – perfectly free,' a voice kept crying within him. It was the least he could do, if he were ever to hold up his head again; but when he opened his mouth to speak not a sound came. At last he halted before Nadeja again, his face working like a frightened child's.

'Nad – what would you like best in the world to do? If you'll tell me I – I want you to do it!' he stammered. And with hands of ice he waited.

Nadeja looked at him with a slowly growing surprise. She had turned very pale again.

'Even if,' he continued, half choking, 'you understand, Nad, even if –'

She continued to look at him in her grave maternal way. 'Is this true, what you are now saying?' she asked very low. Targatt nodded.

A little smile wavered over her lips. 'Well, darling, if only I could have got Mouna safely married, I should have said: Don't you think that now at last we could afford to have a baby?'

POMEGRANATE SEED

I

Charlotte Ashby paused on her doorstep. Dark had descended on the brilliancy of the March afternoon, and the grinding rasping street life of the city was at its highest. She turned her back on it, Standing for a moment in the old-fashioned, marble-flagged vestibule before she inserted her key in the lock. The sash curtains drawn across the panes of the inner door softened the light within to a warm blur through which no details showed. It was the hour when, in the first months of her marriage to Kenneth Ashby, she had most liked to return to that quiet house in a street long since deserted by business and fashion. The contrast between the soulless roar of New York, its devouring blaze of lights, the oppression of its congested traffic, congested houses, lives, minds and this veiled sanctuary she called home, always stirred her profoundly. In the very heart of the hurricane she had found her tiny islet – or thought she had. And now, in the last months, everything was changed, and she always wavered on the door-step and had to force herself to enter.

While she stood there she called up the scene within: the hall hung with old prints, the ladderlike stairs, and on the left her husband's long shabby library, full of books and pipes and worn armchairs inviting to meditation. How she had loved that room! Then, upstairs, her own drawing-room, in which, since the death of Kenneth's first wife, neither furniture nor hangings had been changed, because there had never been money enough, but which Charlotte had made her own by moving furniture about and adding more books, another lamp, a table for the new reviews. Even on the occasion of her only visit to the first Mrs. Ashby – a distant, self-centred woman, whom she had known very slightly – she had looked about her with an innocent envy, feeling it to be exactly the drawing-room she would have liked for herself; and now for more than a year it had been hers to deal with as she chose – the room to which she hastened back at dusk on winter days, where she sat reading by the fire, or answering notes at the pleasant roomy desk, or going over her stepchildren's copy books, till she heard her husband's step.

Sometimes friends dropped in; sometimes – oftener – she was alone; and she liked that best, since it was another way of being with Kenneth, thinking over what he had said when they parted in the morning, imagining what he would say when he sprang up the stairs, found her by herself and caught her to him.

Now, instead of this, she thought of one thing only – the letter she might or might not find on the hall table. Until she had made sure whether or not it was there, her mind had no room for anything else. The letter was always the same – a Square grayish envelope with 'Kenneth Ashby, Esquire.,' written on it in bold but faint characters. From the first it had Struck Charlotte as peculiar that anyone who wrote such a firm hand should trace the letters so lightly; the address was always written as though there were not enough ink in the pen, or the writer's wrist were too weak to bear upon it. Another curious thing was that, in spite of its masculine curves, the writing was so visibly feminine. Some hands are sexless, some masculine, at first glance; the writing on the gray envelope, for all its strength and assurance, was without doubt a woman's. The envelope never bore anything but the recipient's name; no stamp, no address. The letter was presumably delivered by hand – but by whose? No doubt it was slipped into the letter box, whence the parlour maid, when she closed the shutters and lit the lights, probably extracted it. At any rate, it was always in the evening, after dark, that Charlotte saw it lying there. She thought of the letter in the singular, as 'it', because, though there had been several since her marriage – seven, to be exact – they were so alike in appearance that they had become merged in one another in her mind, become one letter, become 'it'.

The first had come the day after their return from their honeymoon – a journey prolonged to the West Indies, from which they had returned to New York after an absence of more than two months. Re-entering the house with her husband, late on that first evening – they had dined at his mother's – she had seen, alone on the hall table, the gray envelope. Her eye fell on it before Kenneth's, and her first thought was: 'Why, I've seen that writing before;' but where she could not recall. The memory was just definite enough for her to identify the Script whenever it looked up at her faintly from the same pale envelope; but on that first day she would have thought no more of the letter if, when her husband's glance lit on it, she had not chanced to be looking at him. It all happened in a flash – his seeing the letter, putting out his hand for it, raising it to his short-sighted eyes to decipher the faint writing, and then abruptly withdrawing the arm he had slipped through Charlotte's, and moving away to the hanging light, his back turned to her. She had waited – waited for a sound, an exclamation; waited for him to open the letter; but he had slipped it into his pocket without a word and followed her into the library. And there they had sat down by the fire and lit their cigarettes, and he had remained silent, his head thrown back broodingly against the armchair, his eyes fixed on the hearth, and presently had passed his hand over his forehead and said: 'Wasn't it unusually hot at my mother's tonight? I've got a splitting head. Mind if I take myself off to bed?'

That was the first time. Since then Charlotte had never been present when he had received the letter. It usually came before he got home from his office, and she had to go upstairs and leave it lying there. But even if she had not seen it, she would have known it had come by the change in his face when he joined her – which, on those evenings, he seldom did before they met for dinner. Evidently, whatever the letter contained, he wanted to be by himself to deal with it; and when he reappeared he looked years older, looked emptied of life and courage, and hardly conscious of her presence. Sometimes he was silent for the rest of the evening; and if he spoke, it was usually to hint some criticism of her household arrangements, suggest some change in the domestic administration, to ask, a little nervously, if she didn't think Joyce's nursery governess was rather young and flighty, or if she herself always saw to it that Peter – whose throat was delicate – was properly wrapped up when he went to school. At such times Charlotte would remember the friendly warnings she had received when she became engaged to Kenneth Ashby: 'Marrying a heartbroken widower! Isn't that rather risky? You know Elsie Ashby absolutely dominated him'; and how she had jokingly replied: 'He may be glad of a little liberty for a change.' And in this respect she had been right. She had needed no one to tell her, during the first months, that her husband was perfectly happy with her. When they came back from their protracted honeymoon the same friends said: 'What have you done to Kenneth? He looks twenty years younger'; and this time she answered with careless joy: 'I suppose I've got him out of his groove.'

But what she noticed after the gray letters began to come was not so much his nervous tentative faultfinding – which always seemed to be uttered against his will – as the look in his eyes when he joined her after receiving one of the letters. The look was not unloving, not even indifferent; it was the look of a man who had been so far away from ordinary events that when he returns to familiar things they seem strange. She minded that more than the faultfinding.

Though she had been sure from the first that the handwriting on the gray envelope was a woman's, it was long before she associated the mysterious letters with any sentimental secret. She was too sure of her husband's love, too confident of filling his life, for such an idea to occur to her. It seemed far more likely that the letters – which certainly did not appear to cause him any sentimental pleasure – were addressed to the busy lawyer than to the private person. Probably they were from some tiresome client – women, he had often hold her, were nearly always tiresome as clients – who did not want her letters opened by his secretary and therefore had them carried to his house. Yes; but in that case the unknown female must be unusually troublesome, judging from the effect her letters produced. Then again, though his professional discretion was exemplary, it was odd that he had never uttered an impatient comment, never remarked to Charlotte, in a moment of expansion, that there was a nuisance of a woman who kept badgering him about a case that had gone against her. He had made more than one semi-confidence of the kind – of course without giving names or details; but concerning this mysterious correspondent his lips were sealed.

There was another possibility: what is euphemistically called an 'old entanglement'. Charlotte Ashby was a sophisticated woman. She had few illusions about the intricacies of the human heart; she knew that there were often old entanglements. But when she had married Kenneth Ashby, her friends, instead of hinting at such a possibility, had said: 'You've got your work cut out for you. Marrying a Don Juan is a sinecure to it. Kenneth's never looked at another woman since he first saw Elsie Corder. During all the years of their marriage he was more like an unhappy lover than a comfortably contented husband. He'll never let you move an armchair or change the place of a lamp; and whatever you venture to do, he'll mentally compare with what Elsie would have done in your place.'

Except for an occasional nervous mistrust as to her ability to manage the children – a mistrust gradually dispelled by her good humour and the children's obvious fondness for her – none of these forebodings had come true. The desolate widower, of whom his nearest friends said that only his absorbing professional interests had kept him from suicide after his first wife's death, had fallen in love, two years later, with Charlotte Gorse, and after an impetuous wooing had married her and carried her off on a tropical honeymoon. And ever since he had been as tender and loverlike as during those first radiant weeks. Before asking her to marry him he had spoken to her frankly of his great love for his first wife and his despair after her sudden death; but even then he had assumed no stricken attitude, or implied that life offered no possibility of renewal. He had been perfectly simple and natural, and had confessed to Charlotte that from the beginning he had hoped the future held new gifts for him. And when, after their marriage, they returned to the house where his twelve years with his first wife had been spent, he had told Charlotte at once that he was sorry he couldn't afford to do the place over for her, but that he knew every woman had her own views about furniture and all sorts of household arrangements a man would never notice, and had begged her to make any changes she saw fit without bothering to consult him. As a result, she made as few as possible; but his way of beginning their new life in the old setting was so frank and unembarrassed that it put her immediately at her ease, and she was almost sorry to find that the Portrait of Elsie Ashby, which used to hang over the desk in his library, had been transferred in their absence to the children's nursery. Knowing herself to be the indirect cause of this banishment, she spoke of it to her husband; but he answered: 'Oh, I thought they ought to grow up with her looking down on them.' The answer moved Charlotte, and satisfied her; and as time went by she had to confess that she felt more at home in her house, more at ease and in confidence with her husband, since that long coldly beautiful face on the library wall no longer followed her with guarded eyes. It was as if Kenneth's love had penetrated to the secret she hardly acknowledged to her own heart – her passionate need to feel herself the sovereign even of his past.

With all this stored-up happiness to sustain her, it was curious that she had lately found herself yielding to a nervous apprehension. But there the apprehension was; and on this particular afternoon – perhaps because she was more tired than usual, or because of the trouble of finding a new cook or, for some other ridiculously trivial reason, moral or physical – she found herself unable to react against the feeling. Latchkey in hand, she looked back down the silent street to the whirl and illumination of the great thoroughfare beyond, and up at the sky already aflare with the city's nocturnal life. 'Outside there,' she thought, 'sky-scrapers, advertisements, telephones, wireless, aeroplanes, movies, motors, and all the rest of the twentieth century; and on the other side of the door something I can't explain, can't relate to them. Something as old as the world, as mysterious as life. . . Nonsense! What am I worrying about? There hasn't been a letter for three months now – not since the day we came back from the country after Christmas. . . Queer that they always seem to come after our holidays! . . . Why should I imagine there's going to be one tonight!'

No reason why, but that was the worst of it – one of the worsts! – that there were days when she would stand there cold and shivering with the premonition of something inexplicable, intolerable, to be faced on the other side of the curtained panes; and when she opened the door and went in, there would be nothing; and on other days when she felt the same premonitory chill, it was justified by the sight of the gray envelope. So that ever since the last had come she had taken to feeling cold and premonitory every evening, because she never opened the door without thinking the letter might be there.

Well, she'd had enough of it; that was certain. She couldn't go on like that. If her husband turned white and had a headache on the days when the letter came, he seemed to recover afterward; but she couldn't. With her the strain had become chronic, and the reason was not far to seek. Her husband knew from whom the letter came and what was in it; he was prepared beforehand for whatever he had to deal with, and master of the situation, however bad; whereas she was shut out in the dark with her conjectures.

'I can't stand it! I can't stand it another day!' she exclaimed aloud, as she put her key in the lock. She turned the key and went in; and there, on the table, lay the letter.

II

She was almost glad of the sight. It seemed to justify everything, to put a seal of definiteness on the whole blurred business. A letter for her husband; a letter from a woman – no doubt another vulgar case of 'old entanglement'. What a fool she had been ever to doubt it, to rack her brains for less obvious explanations! She took up the envelope with a steady contemptuous hand, looked closely at the faint letters, held it against the light and just discerned the outline of the folded sheet within. She knew that now she would have no peace till she found out what was written on that sheet.

Her husband had not come in; he seldom got back from his office before half-past six or seven, and it was not yet six. She would have time to take the letter up to the drawing-room, hold it over the tea-kettle which at that hour always simmered by the fire in expectation of her return, solve the mystery and replace the letter where she had found it. No one would be the wiser, and her gnawing uncertainty would be over. The alternative, of course, was to question her husband; but to do that seemed even more difficult. She weighed the letter between thumb and finger, looked at it again under the light, started up the stairs with the envelope – and came down again and laid it on the table.

'No, I evidently can't,' she said, disappointed.

What should she do, then? She couldn't go up alone to that warm welcoming room, pour out her tea, look over her correspondence, glance at a book or review – not with that letter lying below and the knowledge that in a little while her husband would come in, open it and turn into the library alone, as he always did on the days when the gray envelope came.

Suddenly she decided. She would wait in the library and see for herself; see what happened between him and the letter when they thought themselves unobserved. She wondered the idea had never occurred to her before. By leaving the door ajar, and sitting in the corner behind it, she could watch him unseen. . . Well, then, she would watch him! She drew a chair into the corner, sat down, her eyes on the crack, and waited.

As far as she could remember, it was the first time she had ever tried to surprise another person's secret, but she was conscious of no compunction. She simply felt as if she were fighting her way through a stifling fog that she must at all costs get out of.

At length she heard Kenneth's latchkey and jumped up. The impulse to rush out and meet him had nearly made her forget why she was there; but she remembered in time and sat down again. From her post she covered the whole range of his movements – saw him enter the hall, draw the key from the door and take off his hat and overcoat. Then he turned to throw his gloves on the hall table, and at that moment he saw the envelope. The light was full on his face, and what Charlotte first noted there was a look of surprise. Evidently he had not expected the letter – had not thought of the possibility of its being there that day. But though he had not expected it, now that he saw it he knew well enough what it contained. He did not open it immediately, but stood motionless, the colour slowly ebbing from his face. Apparently he could not make up his mind to touch it; but at length he put out his hand, opened the envelope, and moved with it to the light. In doing so he turned his back on Charlotte, and she saw only his bent head and slightly stooping shoulders. Apparently all the writing was on one page, for he did not turn the sheet but continued to stare at it for so long that he must have reread it a dozen times – or so it seemed to the woman breathlessly watching him. At length she saw him move; he raised the letter still closer to his eyes, as though he had not fully deciphered it. Then he lowered his head, and she saw his lips touch the sheet.

'Kenneth!' she exclaimed, and went out into the hall.

The letter clutched in his hand, her husband turned and looked at her. 'Where were you?' he said, in a low bewildered voice, like a man waked out of his sleep.

'In the library, waiting for you.' She tried to steady her voice: 'What's the matter! What's in that letter? You look ghastly.'

Her agitation seemed to calm him, and he instantly put the envelope into his pocket with a slight laugh. 'Ghastly? I'm sorry. I've had a hard day in the office – one or two complicated cases. I look dogtired, I suppose.'

'You didn't look tired when you came in. It was only when you opened that letter –'

He had followed her into the library, and they stood gazing at each other. Charlotte noticed how quickly he had regained his self-control; his profession had trained him to rapid mastery of face and voice. She saw at once that she would be at a disadvantage in any attempt to surprise his secret, but at the same moment she lost all desire to manoeuvre, to trick him into betraying anything he wanted to conceal. Her wish was still to penetrate the mystery, but only that she might help him to bear the burden it implied. 'Even if it *is* another woman,' she thought.

'Kenneth,' she said, her heart beating excitedly, 'I waited here on purpose to see you come in. I wanted to watch you while you opened that letter.'

His face, which had paled, turned to dark red; then it paled again. 'That letter? Why especially that letter?'

'Because I've noticed that whenever one of those letters comes it seems to have such a strange effect on you.'

A line of anger she had never seen before came out between his eyes, and she said to herself: 'The upper part of his face is too narrow; this is the first time I ever noticed it.'

She heard him continue, in the cool and faintly ironic tone of the prosecuting lawyer making a point: 'Ah; so you're in the habit of watching people open their letters when they don't know you're there?'

'Not in the habit. I never did such a thing before. But I had to find out what she writes to you, at regular intervals, in those gray envelopes.'

He weighed this for a moment; then: 'The intervals have not been regular,' he said.

'Oh, I daresay you've kept a better account of the dates than I have,' she retorted, her magnanimity vanishing at his tone. 'All I know is that every time that woman writes to you –'

'Why do you assume it's a woman?'

'It's a woman's writing. Do you deny it?'

He smiled. 'No, I don't deny it. I asked only because the writing is generally supposed to look more like a man's.'

Charlotte passed this over impatiently. 'And this woman – what does she write to you about?'

Again he seemed to consider a moment. 'About business.'

'Legal business?'

'In a way, yes. Business in general.'

'You look after her affairs for her?'

'Yes.'

'You've looked after them for a long time?'

'Yes. A very long time.'

'Kenneth, dearest, won't you tell me who she is?'

'No. I can't.' He paused, and brought out, as if with a certain hesitation: 'Professional secrecy.'

The blood rushed from Charlotte's heart to her temples. 'Don't say that – don't!'

'Why not?'

'Because I saw you kiss the letter.'

The effect of the words was so disconcerting that she instantly repented having spoken them. Her husband, who had submitted to her cross-questioning with a sort of contemptuous composure, as though he were humouring an unreasonable child, turned on her a face of terror and distress. For a minute he seemed unable to speak; then, collecting himself with an effort, he stammered out: 'The writing is very faint; you must have seen me holding the letter close to my eyes to try to decipher it.'

'No; I saw you kissing it.' He was silent. 'Didn't I see you kissing it?'

He sank back into indifference. 'Perhaps.'

'Kenneth! You stand there and say that – to me?'

'What possible difference can it make to you? The letter is on business, as I told you. Do you suppose I'd lie about it? The writer is a very old friend whom I haven't seen for a long time.'

'Men don't kiss business letters, even from women who are very old friends, unless they have been their lovers, and still regret them.'

He shrugged his Shoulders slightly and turned away, as if he considered the discussion at an end and were faintly disgusted at the turn it had taken.

'Kenneth!' Charlotte moved toward him and caught hold of his arm.

He paused with a look of weariness and laid his hand over hers. 'Won't you believe me?' he asked gently.

'How can I? I've watched these letters come to you – for months now they've been Coming. Ever since we came back from the West Indies – one of them greeted me the very day we arrived. And after each one of them I see their mysterious effect on you, I see you disturbed, unhappy, as if someone were trying to estrange you from me.'

'No, dear; not that. Never!'

She drew back and looked at him with passionate entreaty. 'Well, then, prove it to me, darling. It's so easy!'

He forced a smile. 'It's not easy to prove anything to a woman who's once taken an idea into her head.'

'You've only got to show me the letter.'

His hand slipped from hers and he drew back and shook his head.

'You won't?'

'I can't.'

'Then the woman who wrote it is your mistress.'

'No, dear. No.'

'Not now, perhaps. I suppose she's trying to get you back, and you're struggling, out of pity for me. My poor Kenneth!'

'I swear to you she never was my mistress.'

Charlotte felt the tears rushing to her eyes. 'Ah, that's worse, then – that's hopeless! The prudent ones are the kind that keep their hold on a man. We all know that.' She lifted her hands and hid her face in them.

Her husband remained silent; he offered neither consolation nor denial, and at length, wiping away her tears, she raised her eyes almost timidly to his.

'Kenneth, think! We've been married such a short time. Imagine what you're making me suffer. You say you can't show me this letter. You refuse even to explain it.'

'I've told you the letter is on business. I will swear to that too.'

'A man will swear to anything to screen a woman. If you want me to believe you, at least tell me her name. If you'll do that, I promise you I won't ask to see the letter.'

There was a long interval of suspense, during which she felt her heart beating against her ribs in quick admonitory knocks, as if warning her of the danger she was incurring.

'I can't,' he said at length.

'Not even her name?'

'No.'

'You can't tell me anything more?'

'No.'

Again a pause; this time they seemed both to have reached the end of their arguments and to be helplessly facing each other across a baffling waste of incomprehension.

Charlotte stood breathing rapidly, her hands against her breast. She felt as if she had run a hard race and missed the goal. She had meant to move her husband and had succeeded only in irritating him; and this error of reckoning seemed to change him into a stranger, a mysterious incomprehensible being whom no argument or entreaty of hers could reach. The curious thing was that she was aware in him of no hostility or even impatience, but only of a remoteness, an inaccessibility, far more difficult to overcome. She felt herself excluded, ignored, blotted out of his life. But after a moment or two, looking at him more calmly, she saw that he was suffering as much as she was. His distant guarded face was drawn with pain; the coming of the gray envelope, though it always cast a shadow, had never marked him as deeply as this discussion with his wife.

Charlotte took heart; perhaps, after all, she had not spent her last shaft. She drew nearer and once more laid her hand on his arm. 'Poor Kenneth! If you knew how sorry I am for you –'

She thought he winced slightly at this expression of sympathy, but he took her hand and pressed it.

'I can think of nothing worse than to be incapable of loving long,' she continued; 'to feel the beauty of a great love and to be too unstable to bear its burden.'

He turned on her a look of wistful reproach. 'Oh, don't say that of me. Unstable!'

She felt herself at last on the right tack, and her voice trembled with excitement as she went on: 'Then what about me and this other woman? Haven't you already forgotten Elsie twice within a year?'

She seldom pronounced his first wife's name; it did not come naturally to her tongue. She flung it out now as if she were flinging some dangerous explosive into the open space between them, and drew back a step, waiting to hear the mine go off.

Her husband did not move; his expression grew sadder, but showed no resentment. 'I have never forgotten Elsie,' he said.

Charlotte could not repress a faint laugh. 'Then, you poor dear, between the three of us –'

'There are not –' he began; and then broke off and put his hand to his forehead.

'Not what?'

'I'm sorry; I don't believe I know what I'm saying. I've got a blinding headache.' He looked wan and furrowed enough for the statement to be true, but she was exasperated by his evasion.

'Ah, yes; the gray-envelope headache!'

She saw the surprise in his eyes. 'I'd forgotten how closely I've been watched,' he said coldly. 'If you'll excuse me, I think I'll go up and try an hour in the dark, to see if I can get rid of this neuralgia.'

She wavered; then she said, with desperate resolution: 'I'm sorry your head aches. But before you go I want to say that sooner or later this question must be settled between us. Someone is trying to separate us, and I don't care what it costs me to find out who it is.' She looked him steadily in the eyes.

'If it costs me your love, I don't care! If I can't have your confidence I don't want anything from you.'

He still looked at her wistfully. 'Give me time.'

'Time for what? It's only a word to say.'

'Time to show you that you haven't lost my love or my confidence.'

'Well, I'm waiting.'

He turned toward the door, and then glanced back hesitatingly. 'Oh, do wait, my love,' he said, and went out of the room.

She heard his tired Step on the stairs and the closing of his bedroom door above. Then she dropped into a chair and buried her face in her folded arms. Her first movement was one of compunction; she seemed to herself to have been hard, unhuman, unimaginative. 'Think of telling him that I didn't care if my insistence cost me his love! The lying rubbish!' She started up to follow him and unsay the meaningless words. But she was checked by a reflection. He had had his way, after all; he had eluded all attacks on his secret, and now he was shut up alone in his room, reading that other woman's letter.

III

She was still reflecting on this when the surprised parlour-maid came in and found her. No, Charlotte said, she wasn't going to dress for dinner; Mr. Ashby didn't want to dine. He was very tired and had gone up to his room to rest; later she would have something brought on a tray to the drawing-room. She mounted the stairs to her bedroom. Her dinner dress was lying on the bed, and at the sight the quiet routine of her daily life took hold of her and she began to feel as if the strange talk she had just had with her husband must have taken place in another world, between two beings who were not Charlotte Gorse and Kenneth Ashby, but phantoms projected by her fevered imagination. She recalled the year since her marriage – her husband's constant devotion; his persistent, almost too insistent tenderness; the feeling he had given her at times of being too eagerly dependent on her, too searchingly close to her, as if there were not air enough between her soul and his. It seemed preposterous, as she recalled all this, that a few moments ago she should have been accusing him of an intrigue with another woman! But, then, what –

Again she was moved by the impulse to go up to him, beg his pardon and try to laugh away the misunderstanding. But she was restrained by the fear of forcing herself upon his privacy. He was troubled and unhappy, oppressed by some grief or fear; and he had shown her that he wanted to fight out his battle alone. It would be wiser, as well as more generous, to respect his wish. Only, how strange, how unbearable, to be there, in the next room to his, and feel herself at the other end of the world! In her nervous agitation she almost regretted not having had the courage to open the letter and put it back on the hall table before he came in. At least she would have known what his secret was, and the bogy might have been laid. For she was beginning now to think of the mystery as something conscious, malevolent: a secret persecution before which he quailed, yet from which he could not free himself. Once or twice in his evasive eyes she thought she had detected a desire for help, an impulse of confession, instantly restrained and suppressed. It was as if he felt she could have helped him if she had known, and yet had been unable to tell her!

There flashed through her mind the idea of going to his mother. She was very fond of old Mrs. Ashby, a firm-fleshed clear-eyed old lady, with an astringent bluntness of speech which responded to the forthright and simple in Charlotte's own nature. There had been a tacit bond between them ever since the day when Mrs. Ashby senior, Coming to lunch for the first time with her new daughter-in-law, had been received by Charlotte downstairs in the library, and glancing up at the empty wall above her son's desk, had remarked laconically: 'Elsie gone, eh?' adding, at Charlotte's murmured explanation: 'Nonsense. Don't have her back. Two's Company.' Charlotte, at this reading of her thoughts, could hardly refrain from exchanging a smile of complicity with her mother-in-law; and it seemed to her now that Mrs. Ashby's almost uncanny directness might pierce to the core of this new mystery. But here again she hesitated, for the idea almost suggested a betrayal. What right had she to call in any one, even so close a relation, to surprise a secret which her husband was trying to keep from her? 'Perhaps, by and by, he'll talk to his mother of his own accord,' she thought, and then ended: 'But what does it matter? He and I must settle it between us.'

She was still brooding over the problem when there was a knock on the door and her husband came in. He was dressed for dinner and seemed surprised to see her sitting there, with her evening dress lying unheeded on the bed.

'Aren't you coming down?'

'I thought you were not well and had gone to bed,' she faltered.

He forced a smile. 'I'm not particularly well, but we'd better go down.' His face, though still drawn, looked calmer than when he had fled upstairs an hour earlier.

'There it is; he knows what's in the letter and has fought his battle out again, whatever it is,' she reflected, 'while I'm still in darkness.' She rang and gave a hurried order that dinner should be served as soon as possible – just a short meal, whatever could be got ready quickly, as both she and Mr. Ashby were rather tired and not very hungry.

Dinner was announced, and they sat down to it. At first neither seemed able to find a word to say; then Ashby began to make conversation with an assumption of ease that was more oppressive than his silence. 'How tired he is! How terribly overtired!' Charlotte said to herself, pursuing her own thoughts while he rambled on about municipal politics, aviation, an exhibition of modern French painting, the health of an old aunt and the installing of the automatic telephone. 'Good heavens, how tired he is!'

When they dined alone they usually went into the library after dinner, and Charlotte curled herself up on the divan with her knitting while he settled down in his armchair under the lamp and lit a pipe. But this evening, by tacit agreement, they avoided the room in which their strange talk had taken place, and went up to Charlotte's drawing-room.

They sat down near the fire, and Charlotte said: 'Your pipe?' after he had put down his hardly tasted coffee.

He shook his head. 'No, not tonight.'

'You must go to bed early; you look terribly tired. I'm sure they overwork you at the office.'

'I suppose we all overwork at times.'

She rose and stood before him with sudden resolution. 'Well, I'm not going to have you use up your strength slaving in that way. It's absurd. I can see you're ill.' She bent over him and laid her hand on his forehead. 'My poor old Kenneth. Prepare to be taken away soon on a long holiday.'

He looked up at her, startled. 'A holiday?'

'Certainly. Didn't you know I was going to carry you off at Easter? We're going to start in a fortnight on a month's voyage to somewhere or other. On any one of the big cruising steamers.' She paused and bent closer, touching his forehead with her lips. 'I'm tired, too, Kenneth.'

He seemed to pay no heed to her last words, but sat, his hands on his knees, his head drawn back a little from her caress, and looked up at her with a stare of apprehension. 'Again? My dear, we can't; I can't possibly go away.'

'I don't know why you say 'again', Kenneth; we haven't taken a real holiday this year.'

'At Christmas we spent a week with the children in the country.'

'Yes, but this time I mean away from the children, from servants, from the house. From everything that's familiar and fatiguing. Your mother will love to have Joyce and Peter with her.'

He frowned and slowly shook his head. 'No, dear; I can't leave them with my mother.'

'Why, Kenneth, how absurd! She adores them. You didn't hesitate to leave them with her for over two months when we went to the West Indies.'

He drew a deep breath and stood up uneasily. 'That was different.'

'Different? Why?'

'I mean, at that time I didn't realise' – He broke off as if to choose his words and then went on: 'My mother adores the children, as you say. But she isn't always very judicious. Grandmothers always spoil children. And she sometimes talks before them without thinking.' He turned to his wife with an almost pitiful gesture of entreaty. 'Don't ask me to, dear.'

Charlotte mused. It was true that the elder Mrs. Ashby had a fearless tongue, but she was the last woman in the world to say or hint anything before her grandchildren at which the most scrupulous parent could take offense. Charlotte looked at her husband in perplexity.

'I don't understand.'

He continued to turn on her the same troubled and entreating gaze. 'Don't try to,' he muttered.

'Not try to?'

'Not now – not yet.' He put up his hands and pressed them against his temples. 'Can't you see that there's no use in insisting? I can't go away, no matter how much I might want to.'

Charlotte still scrutinised him gravely. 'The question is, *do* you want to?'

He returned her gaze for a moment; then his lips began to tremble, and he said, hardly above his breath: 'I want – anything you want.'

'And yet –'

'Don't ask me. I can't leave – I can't!'

'You mean that you can't go away out of reach of those letters!'

Her husband had been standing before her in an uneasy half-hesitating attitude; now he turned abruptly away and walked once or twice up and down the length of the room, his head bent, his eyes fixed on the carpet.

Charlotte felt her resentfulness rising with her fears. 'It's that,' she persisted. 'Why not admit it? You can't live without them.'

He continued his troubled pacing of the room; then he stopped short, dropped into a chair and covered his face with his hands. From the shaking of his shoulders, Charlotte saw that he was weeping. She had never seen a man cry, except her father after her mother's death, when she was a little girl; and she remembered still how the sight had frightened her. She was frightened now; she felt that her husband was being dragged away from her into some mysterious bondage, and that she must use up her last atom of strength in the struggle for his freedom, and for hers.

'Kenneth – Kenneth!' she pleaded, kneeling down beside him. 'Won't you listen to me? Won't you try to see what I'm suffering? I'm not unreasonable, darling; really not. I don't suppose I should ever have noticed the letters if it hadn't been for their effect on you. It's not my way to pry into other people's affairs; and even if the effect had been different – yes, yes; listen to me – if I'd seen that the letters made you happy, that you were watching eagerly for them, counting the days between their coming, that you wanted them, that they gave you something I haven't known how to give – why, Kenneth, I don't say I shouldn't have suffered from that, too; but it would have been in a different way, and I should have had the courage to hide what I felt, and the hope that some day you'd come to feel about me as you did about the writer of the letters. But what I can't bear is to see how you dread them, how they make you suffer, and yet how you can't live without them and won't go away lest you should miss one during your absence. Or perhaps,' she added, her voice breaking into a cry of accusation – 'perhaps it's because she's actually forbidden you to leave. Kenneth, you must answer me! Is that the reason? Is it because she's forbidden you that you won't go away with me?'

She continued to kneel at his side, and raising her hands, she drew his gently down. She was ashamed of her persistence, ashamed of uncovering that baffled disordered face, yet resolved that no such scruples should arrest her. His eyes were lowered, the muscles of his face quivered; she was making him suffer even more than she suffered herself. Yet this no longer restrained her.

'Kenneth, is it that? She won't let us go away together?'

Still he did not speak or turn his eyes to her; and a sense of defeat swept over her. After all, she thought, the struggle was a losing one. 'You needn't answer. I see I'm right,' she said.

Suddenly, as she rose, he turned and drew her down again. His hands caught hers and pressed them so tightly that she felt her rings cutting into her flesh. There was something frightened, convulsive in his hold; it was the clutch of a man who felt himself slipping over a precipice. He was staring up at her now as if salvation lay in the face she bent above him. 'Of course we'll go away together. We'll go wherever you want,' he said in a low confused voice; and putting his arm about her, he drew her close and pressed his lips on hers.

IV

Charlotte had said to herself: 'I shall sleep tonight,' but instead she sat before her fire into the small hours, listening for any sound that came from her husband's room. But he, at any rate, seemed to be resting after the tumult of the evening. Once or twice she stole to the door and in the faint light that came in from the street through his open window she saw him stretched out in heavy sleep – the sleep of weakness and exhaustion. 'He's ill,' she thought – 'he's undoubtedly ill. And it's not overwork; it's this mysterious persecution.'

She drew a breath of relief. She had fought through the weary fight and the victory was hers – at least for the moment. If only they could have started at once – started for anywhere! She knew it would be useless to ask him to leave before the holidays; and meanwhile the secret influence – as to which she was still so completely in the dark – would continue to work against her, and she would have to renew the struggle day after day till they started on their journey. But after that everything would be different. If once she could get her husband away under other skies, and all to herself, she never doubted her power to release him from the evil spell he was under. Lulled to quiet by the thought, she too slept at last.

When she woke, it was long past her usual hour, and she sat up in bed surprised and vexed at having overslept herself. She always liked to be down to share her husband's breakfast by the library fire; but a glance at the clock made it clear that he must have started long since for his office. To make sure, she jumped out of bed and went into his room; but it was empty. No doubt he had looked in on her before leaving, seen that she still slept, and gone downstairs without disturbing her; and their relations were sufficiently loverlike for her to regret having missed their morning hour.

She rang and asked if Mr. Ashby had already gone. Yes, nearly an hour ago, the maid said. He had given orders that Mrs. Ashby should not be waked and that the children should not come to her till she sent for them. . . Yes, he had gone up to the nursery himseif to give the order. All this sounded usual enough; and Charlotte hardly knew why she asked: 'And did Mr. Ashby leave no other message?'

Yes, the maid said, he did; she was so sorry she'd forgotten. He'd told her, just as he was leaving, to say to Mrs. Ashby that he was going to see about their passages, and would she please be ready to sail tomorrow?

Charlotte echoed the woman's 'Tomorrow,' and sat staring at her incredulously. 'Tomorrow – you're sure he said to sail tomorrow?'

'Oh, ever so sure, ma'am. I don't know how I could have forgotten to mention it.'

'Well, it doesn't matter. Draw my bath, please.' Charlotte sprang up, dashed through her dressing, and caught herself singing at her image in the glass as she sat brushing her hair. It made her feel young again to have scored such a victory. The other woman vanished to a speck on the horizon, as this one, who ruled the foreground, smiled back at the reflection of her lips and eyes. He loved her, then – he loved her as passionately as ever. He had divined what she had suffered, had understood that their happiness depended on their getting away at once, and finding each other again after yesterday's desperate groping in the fog. The nature of the influence that had come between them did not much matter to Charlotte now; she had faced the phantom and dispelled it. 'Courage – that's the secret! If only people who are in love weren't always so afraid of risking their happiness by looking it in the eyes.' As she brushed back her light abundant hair it waved electrically above her head, like the palms of victory. Ah, well, some women knew how to manage men, and some didn't – and only the fair – she gaily paraphrased – deserve the brave! Certainly she was looking very pretty.

The morning danced along like a cockleshell on a bright sea – such a sea as they would soon be speeding over. She ordered a particularly good dinner, saw the children off to their classes, had her trunks brought down, consulted with the maid about getting out summer clothes – for of course they would be heading for heat and sunshine – and wondered if she oughtn't to take Kenneth's flannel suits out of camphor. 'But how absurd,' she reflected, 'that I don't yet know where we're going!' She looked at the clock, saw that it was close on noon, and decided to call him up at his office. There was a slight delay; then she heard his secretary's voice saying that Mr. Ashby had looked in for a moment early, and left again almost immediately. . . Oh, very well; Charlotte would ring up later. How soon was he likely to be back? The secretary answered that she couldn't tell; all they knew in the office was that when he left he had said he was in a hurry because he had to go out of town.

Out of town! Charlotte hung up the receiver and sat blankly gazing into new darkness. Why had he gone out of town? And where had he gone? And of all days, why should he have chosen the eve of their suddenly planned departure? She felt a faint shiver of apprehension. Of course he had gone to see that woman – no doubt to get her permission to leave. He was as completely in bondage as that; and Charlotte had been fatuous enough to see the palms of victory on her forehead. She burst into a laugh and, walking across the room, sat down again before her mirror. What a different face she saw! The smile on her pale lips seemed to mock the rosy vision of the other Charlotte. But gradually her colour crept back. After all, she had a right to claim the victory, since her husband was doing what she wanted, not what the other woman exacted of him. It was natural enough, in view of his abrupt decision to leave the next day, that he should have arrangements to make, business matters to wind up; it was not even necessary to suppose that his mysterious trip was a visit to the writer of the letters. He might simply have gone to see a client who lived out of town. Of course they would not tell Charlotte at the office; the secretary had hesitated before imparting even such meagre information as the fact of Mr. Ashby's absence. Meanwhile she would go on with her joyful preparations, content to learn later in the day to what particular island of the blest she was to be carried.

The hours wore on, or rather were swept forward on a rush of eager preparations. At last the entrance of the maid who came to draw the curtains roused Charlotte from her labours, and she saw to her surprise that the clock marked five. And she did not yet know where they were going the next day! She rang up her husband's office and was told that Mr. Ashby had not been there since the early morning. She asked for his partner, but the partner could add nothing to her information, for he himself, his suburban train having been behind time, had reached the office after Ashby had come and gone. Charlotte stood perplexed; then she decided to telephone to her mother-in-law. Of course Kenneth, on the eve of a month's absence, must have gone to see his mother. The mere fact that the children – in spite of his vague objections – would certainly have to be left with old Mrs. Ashby, made it obvious that he would have all sorts of matters to decide with her. At another time Charlotte might have felt a little hurt at being excluded from their conference, but nothing mattered now but that she had won the day, that her husband was still hers and not another woman's. Gaily she called up Mrs. Ashby, heard her friendly voice, and began: 'Well, did Kenneth's news surprise you? What do you think of our elopement?'

Almost instantly, before Mrs. Ashby could answer, Charlotte knew what her reply would be. Mrs. Ashby had not seen her son, she had had no word from him and did not know what her daughter-in-law meant. Charlotte stood silent in the intensity of her surprise. 'But then, where *has* he been?' she thought. Then, recovering herself, she explained their sudden decision to Mrs. Ashby, and in doing so, gradually regained her own self-confidence, her conviction that nothing could ever again come between Kenneth and herself. Mrs. Ashby took the news calmly and approvingly. She, too, had thought that Kenneth looked worried and overtired, and she agreed with her daughter-in-law that in such cases change was the surest remedy. 'I'm always so glad when he gets away. Elsie hated travelling; she was always finding pretexts to prevent his going anywhere. With you, thank goodness, it's different.' Nor was Mrs. Ashby surprised at his not having had time to let her know of his departure. He must have been in a rush from the moment the decision was taken; but no doubt he'd drop in before dinner. Five minutes' talk was really all they needed. 'I hope you'll gradually cure Kenneth of his mania for going over and over a question that could be settled in a dozen words. He never used to be like that, and if he carried the habit into his professional work he'd soon lose all his clients. . . Yes, do come in for a minute, dear, if you have time; no doubt he'll turn up while you're here.' The tonic ring of Mrs. Ashby's voice echoed on reassuringly in the silent room while Charlotte continued her preparations.

Toward seven the telephone rang, and she darted to it. Now she would know! But it was only from the conscientious secretary, to say that Mr. Ashby hadn't been back, or sent any word, and before the office closed she thought she ought to let Mrs. Ashby know. 'Oh, that's all right. Thanks a lot!' Charlotte called out cheerfully, and hung up the receiver with a trembling hand. But perhaps by this time, she reflected, he was at his mother's. She shut her drawers and cupboards, put on her hat and coat and called up to the nursery that she was going out for a minute to see the children's grandmother.

Mrs. Ashby lived near by, and during her brief walk through the cold spring dusk Charlotte imagined that every advancing figure was her husband's. But she did not meet him on the way, and when she entered the house she found her mother-in-law alone. Kenneth had neither telephoned nor come. Old Mrs. Ashby sat by her bright fire, her knitting needles flashing steadily through her active old hands, and her mere bodily presence gave reassurance to Charlotte. Yes, it was certainly odd that Kenneth had gone off for the whole day without letting any of them know; but, after all, it was to be expected. A busy lawyer held so many threads in his hands that any sudden change of plan would oblige him to make all sorts of unforeseen arrangements and adjustments. He might have gone to see some client in the suburbs and been detained there; his mother remembered his telling her that he had Charge of the legal business of a queer old recluse somewhere in New Jersey, who was immensely rich but too mean to have a telephone. Very likely Kenneth had been stranded there.

But Charlotte felt her nervousness gaining on her. When Mrs. Ashby asked her at what hour they were sailing the next day and she had to say she didn't know – that Kenneth had simply sent her word he was going to take their passages – the uttering of the words again brought home to her the strangeness of the situation. Even Mrs. Ashby conceded that it was odd; but she immediately added that it only showed what a rush he was in.

'But, mother, it's nearly eight o'clock! He must realise that I've got to know when we're starting tomorrow.'

'Oh, the boat probably doesn't sail till evening. Sometimes they have to wait till midnight for the tide. Kenneth's probably counting on that. After all, he has a level head.'

Charlotte stood up. 'It's not that. Something has happened to him.'

Mrs. Ashby took off her spectacles and rolled up her knitting. 'If you begin to let yourself imagine things –'

'Aren't you in the least anxious?'

'I never am till I have to be. I wish you'd ring for dinner, my dear. You'll stay and dine? He's sure to drop in here on his way home.'

Charlotte called up her own house. No, the maid said, Mr. Ashby hadn't come in and hadn't telephoned. She would tell him as soon as he came that Mrs. Ashby was dining at his mother's. Charlotte followed her mother-in-law into the dining-room and sat with parched throat before her empty plate, while Mrs. Ashby dealt calmly and efficiently with a short but carefully prepared repast. 'You'd better eat something, child, or you'll be as bad as Kenneth. . . Yes, a little more asparagus, please, Jane.'

She insisted on Charlotte's drinking a glass of Sherry and nibbling a bit of toast; then they returned to the drawing-room, where the fire had been made up, and the cushions in Mrs. Ashby's armchair shaken out and smoothed. How safe and familiar it all looked; and out there, somewhere in the uncertainty and mystery of the night, lurked the answer to the two women's conjectures, like an indistinguishable figure prowling on the threshold.

At last Charlotte got up and said: 'I'd better go back. At this hour Kenneth will certainly go straight home.'

Mrs. Ashby smiled indulgently. 'It's not very late, my dear. It doesn't take two sparrows long to dine.'

'It's after nine.' Charlotte bent down to kiss her. 'The fact is, I can't keep still.'

Mrs. Ashby pushed aside her work and rested her two hands on the arms of her chair. 'I'm going with you,' she said, helping herself up.

Charlotte protested that it was too late, that it was not necessary, that she would call up as soon as Kenneth came in, but Mrs. Ashby had already rung for her maid. She was slightly lame, and stood resting on her stick while her wraps were brought. 'If Mr. Kenneth turns up, tell him he'll find me at his own house,' she instructed the maid as the two women got into the taxi which had been summoned. During the short drive Charlotte gave thanks that she was not returning home alone. There was something warm and substantial in the mere fact of Mrs. Ashby's nearness, something that corresponded with the clearness of her eyes and the texture of her fresh firm complexion. As the taxi drew up she laid her hand encouragingly on Charlotte's. 'You'll see; there'll be a message.'

The door opened at Charlotte's ring and the two entered. Charlotte's heart beat excitedly; the stimulus of her mother-in-law's confidence was beginning to flow through her veins.

'You'll see – you'll see,' Mrs. Ashby repeated.

The maid who opened the door said no, Mr. Ashby had not come in, and there had been no message from him.

'You're sure the telephone's not out of order?' his mother suggested; and the maid said, well, it certainly wasn't half an hour ago; but she'd just go and ring up to make sure. She disappeared, and Charlotte turned to take off her hat and cloak. As she did so her eyes lit on the hall table, and there lay a gray envelope, her husband's name faintly traced on it. 'Oh!' she cried out, suddenly aware that for the first time in months she had entered her house without wondering if one of the gray letters would be there.

'What is it, my dear?' Mrs. Ashby asked with a glance of surprise.

Charlotte did not answer. She took up the envelope and stood staring at it as if she could force her gaze to penetrate to what was within. Then an idea occurred to her. She turned and held out the envelope to her mother-in-law.

'Do you know that writing?' she asked.

Mrs. Ashby took the letter. She had to feel with her other hand for her eyeglasses, and when she had adjusted them she lifted the envelope to the light. 'Why!' she exclaimed; and then stopped. Charlotte noticed that the letter shook in her usually firm hand. 'But this is addressed to Kenneth,' Mrs. Ashby said at length, in a low voice. Her tone seemed to imply that she felt her daughter-in-law's question to be slightly indiscreet.

'Yes, but no matter,' Charlotte spoke with sudden decision, 'I want to know – do you know the writing?'

Mrs. Ashby handed back the letter. 'No,' she said distinctly.

The two women had turned into the library. Charlotte switched on the electric light and shut the door. She still held the envelope in her hand.

'I'm going to open it,' she announced.

She caught her mother-in-law's startled glance. 'But, dearest – a letter not addressed to you? My dear, you can't!'

'As if I cared about that – now!' She continued to look intently at Mrs. Ashby. 'This letter may tell me where Kenneth is.'

Mrs. Ashby's glossy bloom was effaced by a quick pallor; her firm cheeks seemed to shrink and wither. 'Why should it? What makes you believe – It can't possibly –'

Charlotte held her eyes steadily on that altered face. 'Ah, then you *do* know the writing?' she flashed back.

'Know the writing? How should I? With all my son's correspondents. . . What I do know is –' Mrs. Ashby broke off and looked at her daughter-in-law entreatingly, almost timidly.

Charlotte caught her by the wrist. 'Mother! What do you know? Tell me! You must!'

'That I don't believe any good ever came of a woman's opening her husband's letters behind his back.'

The words sounded to Charlotte's irritated ears as flat as a phrase culled from a book of moral axioms. She laughed impatiently and dropped her mother-in-law's wrist. 'Is that all? No good can come of this letter, opened or unopened. I know that well enough. But whatever ill comes, I mean to find out what's in it.' Her hands had been trembling as they held the envelope, but now they grew firm, and her voice also. She still gazed intently at Mrs. Ashby. 'This is the ninth letter addressed in the same hand that has come for Kenneth since we've been married. Always these same gray envelopes. I've kept count of them because after each one he has been like a man who has had some dreadful shock. It takes him hours to shake off their effect. I've told him so. I've told him I must know from whom they come, because I can see they're killing him. He won't answer my questions; he says he can't tell me anything about the letters; but last night he promised to go away with me – to get away from them.'

Mrs. Ashby, with shaking steps, had gone to one of the armchairs and sat down in it, her head drooping forward on her breast. 'Ah,' she murmured.

'So now you understand –'

'Did he tell you it was to get away from them?'

'He said, to get away – to get away. He was sobbing so that he could hardly speak. But I told him I knew that was why.'

'And what did he say?'

'He took me in his arms and said he'd go wherever I wanted.'

'Ah, thank God!' said Mrs. Ashby. There was a silence, during which she continued to sit with bowed head, and eyes averted from her daughter-in-law. At last she looked up and spoke. 'Are you sure there have been as many as nine?'

'Perfectly. This is the ninth. I've kept count.'

'And he has absolutely refused to explain?'

'Absolutely.'

Mrs. Ashby spoke through pale contracted lips. 'When did they begin to come? Do you remember?'

Charlotte laughed again. 'Remember? The first one came the night we got back from our honeymoon.'

'All that time?' Mrs. Ashby lifted her head and spoke with sudden energy. 'Then – Yes, open it.'

The words were so unexpected that Charlotte felt the blood in her temples, and her hands began to tremble again. She tried to slip her finger under the flap of the envelope, but it was so tightly stuck that she had to hunt on her husband's writing table for his ivory letter-opener. As she pushed about the familiar objects his own hands had so lately touched, they sent through her the icy chill emanating from the little personal effects of someone newly dead. In the deep silence of the room the tearing of the paper as she slit the envelope sounded like a human cry. She drew out the sheet and carried it to the lamp.

'Well?' Mrs. Ashby asked below her breath.

Charlotte did not move or answer. She was bending over the page with wrinkled brows, holding it nearer and nearer to the light. Her sight must be blurred, or else dazzled by the reflection of the lamplight on the smooth surface of the paper, for, strain her eyes as she would, she could discern only a few faint strokes, so faint and faltering as to be nearly undecipherable.

'I can't make it out,' she said.

'What do you mean, dear?'

'The writing's too indistinct... Wait.'

She went back to the table and, sitting down close to Kenneth's reading lamp, slipped the letter under a magnifying glass. All this time she was aware that her mother-in-law was watching her intently.

'Well?' Mrs. Ashby breathed.

'Well, it's no clearer. I can't read it.'

'You mean the paper is an absolute blank?'

'No, not quite. There is writing on it. I can make out something like 'mine' – oh, and 'come'. It might be 'come'.'

Mrs. Ashby stood up abruptly. Her face was even paler than before. She advanced to the table and, resting her two hands on it, drew a deep breath. 'Let me see,' she said, as if forcing herself to a hateful effort.

Charlotte felt the contagion of her whiteness. 'She knows,' she thought. She pushed the letter across the table. Her mother-in-law lowered her head over it in silence, but without touching it with her pale wrinkled hands.

Charlotte stood watching her as she herself, when she had tried to read the letter, had been watched by Mrs. Ashby. The latter fumbled for her glasses, held them to her eyes, and bent still closer to the outspread page, in order, as it seemed, to avoid touching it. The light of the lamp fell directly on her old face, and Charlotte reflected what depths of the unknown may lurk under the clearest and most candid lineaments. She had never seen her mother-in-law's features express any but simple and sound emotions – cordiality, amusement, a kindly sympathy; now and again a flash of wholesome anger. Now they seemed to wear a look of fear and hatred, of incredulous dismay and almost cringing defiance. It was as if the spirits warring within her had distorted her face to their own likeness. At length she raised her head. 'I can't – I can't,' she said in a voice of childish distress.

'You can't make it out either?'

She shook her head, and Charlotte saw two tears roll down her cheeks.

'Familiar as the writing is to you?' Charlotte insisted with twitching lips.

Mrs. Ashby did not take up the challenge. 'I can make out nothing – nothing.'

'But you do know the writing?'

Mrs. Ashby lifted her head timidly; her anxious eyes stole with a glance of apprehension around the quiet familiar room. 'How can I tell? I was startled at first. . .'

'Startled by the resemblance?'

'Well. I thought –'

'You'd better say it out, mother! You knew at once it was *her* writing?'

'Oh, wait, my dear – wait.'

'Wait for what?'

Mrs. Ashby looked up; her eyes, travelling slowly past Charlotte, were lifted to the blank wall behind her son's writing table.

Charlotte, following the glance, burst into a shrill laugh of accusation. 'I needn't wait any longer! You've answered me now! You're looking straight at the wall where her picture used to hang!'

Mrs. Ashby lifted her hand with a murmur of warning. 'Sh-h.'

'Oh, you needn't imagine that anything can ever frighten me again!' Charlotte cried.

Her mother-in-law still leaned against the table. Her lips moved plaintively. 'But we're going mad – we're both going mad. We both know such things are impossible.'

Her daughter-in-law looked at her with a pitying stare. 'I've known for a long time now that everything was possible.'

'Even this?'

'Yes, exactly this.'

'But this letter – after all, there's nothing in this letter –'

'Perhaps there would be to him. How can I tell? I remember his saying to me once that if you were used to a handwriting the faintest stroke of it became legible. Now I see what he meant. He *was* used to it.'

'But the few strokes that I can make out are so pale. No one could possibly read that letter.'

Charlotte laughed again. 'I suppose everything's pale about a ghost,' she said stridently.

'Oh, my child – my child – don't say it!'

'Why shouldn't I say it, when even the bare walls cry it out? What difference does it make if her letters are illegible to you and me? If even you can see her face on that blank wall, why shouldn't he read her writing on this blank paper? Don't you see that she's everywhere in this house, and the closer to him because to everyone else she's become invisible?' Charlotte dropped into a chair and covered her face with her hands. A turmoil of sobbing shook her from head to foot. At length a touch on her shoulder made her look up, and she saw her mother-in-law bending over her. Mrs. Ashby's face seemed to have grown still smaller and more wasted, but it had resumed its usual quiet look. Through all her tossing anguish, Charlotte felt the impact of that resolute spirit.

'Tomorrow – tomorrow. You'll see. There'll be some explanation tomorrow.'

Charlotte cut her short. 'An explanation? Who's going to give it, I wonder?'

Mrs. Ashby drew back and straightened herself heroically. 'Kenneth himself will,' she cried out in a strong voice. Charlotte said nothing, and the old woman went on: 'But meanwhile we must act; we must notify the police. Now, without a moment's delay. We must do everything – everything.'

Charlotte stood up slowly and stiffly; her joints felt as cramped as an old woman's. 'Exactly as if we thought it could do any good to do anything?'

Resolutely Mrs. Ashby cried: 'Yes!' and Charlotte went up to the telephone and unhooked the receiver.

PERMANENT WAVE*

I

It gave Mrs. Vincent Craig a cold shiver to think how nearly she had missed her turn at Gaston's. Two women were already in the outer room, waiting to be waved, when she rushed in – 'late as usual' (as her husband always said, in that irritating level voice of his).

The hair-dresser looked at her with astonishment.

'But I expected you yesterday, Mrs. Craig.'

'Yesterday? Oh, that's a mistake. . . I've got it written down here.' She plunged into her bag for her engagement-book, but brought up only a passport and a bunch of travellers' cheques, which she didn't want seen, and thrust back hurriedly.

'I must have left my book at home. But I have the day written down. . .'

The busy hair-dresser shrugged. 'So have I. But anyhow your appointment was for two.'

'Well, what time is it now? Only a quarter past.' After that it had taken all her arguments, persuasions, feigned indignations, fawning flattery even, to persuade the illustrious hair-dresser that he had no right, absolutely no right, to give away her appointment simply because she was a few minutes late ('Oh, half an hour? Really, Gaston, you exaggerate! Look at my watch . . . well, it was my husband who gave me that watch. Do you wonder if it's sometimes a little slow?'). And finally, with a faint conniving

* *Originally published under the title: Poor Old Vincent.*

smile, and a shrug at the two fuming women in the background, the artist had let Mrs. Craig slip into the tiled sanctuary.

Oh, the relief – the release from that cold immediate menace! It ran down Nalda Craig in little streams of retrospective fear, as if she had been sleep-walking, and suddenly opened her eyes just as she hung above a precipice. Think of it! If she had had to join Phil Ingerson at the station the next morning with a mop of lank irregular hair – for it wanted cutting as well as waving; and goodness knows, in the end-of-the-world places he and she were bound for, how soon she'd have another chance of being properly 'done'. Ah, how she'd always envied women with a natural wave! No difficulty for *them* in eloping with explorers. Of course they had to undergo the waving ordeal now and then too, but not nearly so often. . . Well, if there were good hair-dressers in Central America, she only hoped Phil wouldn't grouse about the expense, as Vincent had always done, playfully at first, then half irritably, then with that thin disparaging smile of his. 'What, another barber's bill? Let's see if you've really been there this time.' For, unless he scrutinised her closely, applied his mind to it, as well as his puzzled unseeing eyes, he never knew if her hair had been newly waved or not.

All the better, perhaps in the present case. For her last wave was only three weeks old, and if Vincent had been a little more observant he might have said, when they met at dinner that evening: 'Hello, hel-lo! Another twenty-dollar ripple already?' And as they were dining alone that night, and she could not dodge behind the general talk, it might have been awkward to explain. But as it was, he would sit there all the evening with his nose in his book, and if she should appear before him with her head shaved instead of waved he would never notice that either.

It was that which had been such a disillusionment when they were first married; his not being at every moment acutely conscious of her looks, her clothes, her graces, of what she was thinking or feeling. More than once she had nearly burst out:

'If you'd only find fault with me!' But on the rare occasions when he did find fault she didn't like that either. Her mother and grandmother had brought her up with such different ideas of a husband's obligations toward his wife. 'My husband was my lover to the very end,' her grandmother used to simper, turning on all her withered dimples; and Nalda's mother, though of course she didn't put it so romantically, always said: 'Whatever your father's faults may have been,' (it was hinted that conviviality was not the only one) 'he was always the chivalrous gentleman where his wife was concerned.'

It all sounded funny and old-fashioned; but if it meant anything at all, it meant, in modern lingo, that your husband was your pal, and that he backed up his little woman through thick and thin, and paid the bills without grumbling. Whereas Nalda had more than once had to borrow money in secret; and when she had that nasty dispute with the dressmaker about the price of her broad-tail coat Vincent hadn't backed up his little woman for a cent...

Well, she had on the broad-tail when she first met Phil Ingerson. It was at that skating-party on the river that the Pressly Normans had got up; and could she help it if she was prettier than the other women, and if her fur coat was out and away the smartest there, and if her hair had been 'permed' the day before, and looked as lustrous as a chestnut just out of the burr? It was funny, perhaps, to date such an overwhelming event as her first encounter with Phil Ingerson by the fact of her having been waved the previous day; but then being waved gave one, as nothing else did, no, not even a new hat, that sense of security and power which a woman never needed more than at her first meeting with the man who was to re-make her life...

II

Funny – she remembered now how bored and restless she used to get during that interminable waving *séance*. Four hours of immobility; 'in the stocks', as Winna Norman called it. When you had run through Gaston's supply of picture papers, and exchanged platitudes with the other victims, if they happened to be acquaintances, there was simply nothing to do but to yawn and fidget, and think of all the worries and bothers which could be kept in abeyance at other times by bridge and golf and tennis, and rushing about, always a little late, to one's engagements. Yes; she had chafed at the imprisonment then: called it 'serving a life sentence'; but since she had known Phil Ingerson (six months it must be, for this was her fourth wave since their first meeting) she had come to look forward to that four hours' immobility as a time for brooding over their friendship, taking stock of herself and of him. No leisure would have seemed too long for that, she thought. She looked at the driven faces of the other women, desperately enduring the four hours' imprisonment with their own thoughts; then she sank back into her secret bath of beatitude. There was so much to occupy her thoughts; every word of Phil's, every glance, his smile, his laugh, his comments on her dress and her looks (*he* never failed to notice when she had been newly waved!), and his odd paradoxical judgments of life and men, which were never exactly what one expected, and therefore so endlessly exciting – whereas with poor Vincent you could tell before he opened his mouth what he was going to say, and say it for him more quickly than he could get it out.

Not that (she interrupted herself parenthetically) she did not appreciate Vincent. Of course she did. She had always appreciated him. She knew how high he stood in his profession, how much the University esteemed him as a lecturer, and as an authority on his particular subject. And of course economics had become such an important branch of learning that Vincent Craig's name was known far beyond the University, and he sat up late writing learned articles for historical reviews and philosophical quarterlies; and she had even, at a New York reception, heard some one to whom she had been pointed out, eagerly rejoin: 'What? The wife of *the* Vincent Craig? Is *he* here, by any chance?'

No one should dare to say she had not appreciated Vincent – she wasn't as stupid as all that! Only, when a man's life is wrapped up in economics, so little is left over for his wife. And had Vincent ever appreciated *her*? Hadn't he always taken her as much for granted as the cook, or the electric light, or the roof over his head? He had never seemed to be aware of her personality; and nothing was as humiliating to a woman as that. When he went out in the morning did it ever occur to him that he might not find his wife at the head of his table when he returned at night? What had he ever known of such palpitating anguish as she felt when, after every parting with Phil, she asked herself: 'Shall I ever see him again?', or of the absurd boyish rapture with which, at every sight of her, Phil would exclaim: 'I thought you were never coming! What on earth has kept you so long?'

Phil, in short, measured his hours by her comings and goings; Vincent measured his by college tasks, professional appointments, literary obligations, or interviewing people about gas and electricity and taxes. The two men lived in different worlds, between which, for the last months, Nalda had been swept on alternating currents of passion and compunction...

For of course – again – she was sorry, by anticipation, for Vincent. He would hate to have her leave him, even though her presence made so little difference – or seemed to. For she could not but remember how, after her bad grippe and pneumonia, he had burst into tears the first day he was re-admitted to her room, and the nurse had had to hurry him out again lest he should 'bring back the fever'. She smiled a little over the memory, self-complacently; and amusedly at the recollection of his re-appearing, the next day, with a two-pound bag of *marrons glacés*, as the appropriate offering to a woman whose palate still shuddered at anything less ethereal than a grape! 'Why, I thought you liked them,' he had stammered. 'Perhaps you'll fancy one later –' and left the sticky nauseating bag on her bed when he went out. . . Old Vincent!

There hadn't been much time to conjecture as to how Phil would behave if she were very ill; but something already whispered to her that she had better not try the experiment. 'He wouldn't know how . . .' she thought; and her lip curled with a sudden sense of their youth and power, and the mysterious security of their passion. . .

III

Of course it was for her, and her alone, that Phil had turned up at Kingsbridge so often during the last months. He said the grave was a circus compared with a University town; and especially a New England University town. West of the Rockies academic life might have a little more ginger in it; but in the very capital of the Cut-and-Dried there was nothing doing for a young fellow of such varied ambitions and subversive views as Phil Ingerson, and he frankly confessed to Nalda that he had dashed down for a week-end with his aunt Miss Marcham (one of the social and financial pillars of the University) only because he was in pursuit, at the moment, of a good-looking girl he had run across on a West Indian cruise, and who kept house for her brother, a Kings-bridge professor. Poor Olive Fresno! – cutting her out had been part of the fun in the early days of Nalda's encounter with Phil. The girl had her points (Nalda was the first to admit it), and she had evidently been thawed out by the easy promiscuities of the cruise. But back under her brother's roof (he was Professor of Comparative Theology) she had turned icicle again, a blushing agonizing icicle, whom it was fun to taunt and tantalise; and to eclipse her with the easily-bored Phil had been a walk-over for Mrs. Craig.

Now, as Nalda sat there, with her Medusa-locks in the steel clutch of the waver, she felt, she couldn't tell why, a sudden pang of compunction about Olive Fresno. It wasn't Nalda's fault, of course, if the first sight of her (yes, that wonderful first day on the ice) had sealed poor Olive's fate. Nalda didn't for a moment imagine that, if she'd behaved differently, the Fresno girl might have got what she wanted; she simply shivered a little at the apparently inevitable cost of happiness. Life was so constituted that when you grabbed what you wanted you always left somebody else to pay the damages. All that was as old as the hills; but it had suddenly turned, in Nalda's mind, from a copy-book axiom into a burning reality. . .

Not indeed in terms of Olive Fresno. The person of whom Nalda was really thinking, under that disguise, was her husband. For the first time in her life she pictured to herself what he would suffer. Once, when she had spoken of it to Phil (just to see if it would make him jealous), he had vexed her by saying with a laugh: 'Suffer – what for? Why shouldn't he marry Olive?'

It was not what she had meant him to say, and she had been distinctly offended. But she herself, at that time, had not been really sorry for her husband; she had simply been using him as a spice to whet Phil's appetite. Now it was different. Now that everything was irrevocably settled, even to the passport in her pocket, she knew for the first time what Vincent was feeling, seemed even, in a queer unexpected way, to be feeling it with him, to be not only the cause of his suffering but a sharer in it. . .

A moment later a reaction of pity for Phil set in. Look at the difference between the careers of the two men! Vincent Craig had gone from achievement to achievement, from one academic honour to another. He had been 'the Vincent Craig' for years now. And Phil (as he had often told her) had had the academic world against him from the start. Even his aunt, with all her influence at Kingsbridge, had never been able to interest the University authorities in what he called his discoveries, and they called his theories. And the articles he had published on his archæological expedition in Central America, which his aunt had financed, had been passed over in silence in high quarters.

The woman nearest to Nalda said to her neighbour on the other side: 'I never choose a day for this but just as I start there's a rumpus at home. This time it's the new girl. . .'

The other responded drearily: 'I don't have to have my hair waved to have trouble with the help.'

There was a long silence. Then one of the two said: 'I see they're going to wear those uncrushable velvets a good deal this winter.'

'Well, all I can say is, mine was a rag when I took it out of the trunk —'

Nalda nestled down again into her own warm dream. Thank heaven she wasn't going to hear any more of that sort of talk — oh, not for ages, she hoped! Not that she wasn't interested in this new uncrushable velvet . . . she rather wished now she'd had her one good dress made of it, instead of a flowered chiffon. But chiffon took up so much less room, and Phil seemed to be as fussy as other men about too much luggage. . . And after all, as they would have to do a good deal of flying. . .

A sudden anxiety stirred in her. Miss Marcham, she knew, had given Phil the new aeroplane in which he was to explore the inaccessible ruins of Yucatan; the expedition which, if successful, would confirm his theory as to the introduction of Oriental culture to the Western hemisphere in — well, she simply never could remember whether it was B.C. something, or very early A.D. And Phil wouldn't mind her not remembering. He said he didn't want to elope with the *Encyclopædia Britannica*; on the contrary. . . Only, if Miss Marcham, who was such an important figure at Kingsbridge, and took such a serious view of her standing in the University world — if Miss Marcham had known that the aeroplane she had paid for was to be used by her nephew to carry off the wife of Professor Vincent Craig. . .

'What I always say is, it pays in the end to get your groceries sent from New York. But of course the cook hates it. . . What they like is to have the grocer calling every day for orders. . .'

Nalda had imparted her scruples about the aeroplane to Phil: but he had only laughed. 'If it's any comfort to you, my dear, I didn't make my first expedition alone. . .' It was no comfort to her, but it silenced her protest. She didn't want him to think her what he called 'Kingsbridgy.' And, after all, to make a fuss about a trifle like an aeroplane, when her leaving was going to shatter a man's life! Yes – Vincent's life would be shattered! That cold current again, through the soft Gulf Stream of her broodings. . .

'Well, when I come here to be waved I always say to myself before I open the door: 'Now, whatever you do, *don't worry*! Because no matter what's going on at home, you can't help it'.'

'No; but it does make it worse to have four hours to think things over.'

Ah, yes; this time the woman was right! Four hours *were* too long to think over a plight like Nalda Craig's. It was never safe to turn any sentiment inside out; and happiness perhaps least of all. Happiness ought to be like a spring breeze blowing in at the window, coming from one didn't know where, bearing the scent of invisible flowers. You couldn't take it to pieces and put it together, like a sum in arithmetic. . . She began to wish the waving were over.

'Well, I think you'll be satisfied with this job, Mrs. Craig,' Gaston said, fluttering her chestnut ripples through his wizard fingers. The other women had been released, and gone their ways, and she had the room to herself, and could smile back complacently at her reflection, without risk of having the smile registered over her shoulder by envious eyes. Yes, she was satisfied! She leaned back and yielded her head to the hair-dresser's rapid manipulations. The four hours didn't seem long now. . .

'Well, I must fly. Oh, here, Gaston –' she drew the twenty dollar bill from her bag. Then, involuntarily, she paused and glanced about the familiar walls of Gaston's operating-room, as Winna Norman called it. It made things look so funny when you knew you were seeing them for the last time. She noticed that the woman next to her had left a box of rouge on the washstand.

Her eyes travelled slowly about the room; then she stopped short with an exclamation.

'Ma'am?' queried Gaston, who was busy with his helper preparing for the next batch of victims.

Nalda gave a nervous laugh. She was pointing to a calendar on the wall. 'You're a day ahead, Gaston.'

He turned and followed her glance.

'Why, no. Today's Thursday.'

She began to tremble inwardly. 'Today's Wednesday, Gaston.'

He shrugged. 'I guess it's you who are behind the times, Mrs. Craig. I always pull off the leaf first thing every morning, myself. I don't trust anybody else to do it.'

'Are you sure it's Thursday?' she repeated, with dry lips, as if he had not spoken. But one of the women she had ousted was coming back, sulkily, to be marcelled; and Gaston was already engaged in installing her.

Nalda walked blindly out of the shop. She did not know she had left it until she heard the door swing to behind her. It was Thursday . . . it was Thursday. . . Gaston said he always pulled the page off the calendar every morning himself. . . Instead of letting days and days pass, as she did, and then tearing off a bunch at haphazard. How often her husband had laughed at her for that! 'Nalda never knows the day of the week. She says it would only cramp her style if she did. . .'

A busy man who kept a shop couldn't afford to be as careless as that. If Gaston said it was Thursday, then it was Thursday.

IV

She walked on unsteadily, deaf and blind to the noise and whirl of the street. She turned out of the business quarter into the residential part of the town without being conscious of the direction she was taking. She seemed to be following her feet instead of being carried by them.

Thursday – but then, if it was Thursday, Phil would have been waiting for her at the station at ten o'clock that morning! Slowly her stunned brain began to take it in. And when the time came for the start, and she was not there – what then? Wouldn't he have rushed to the house, or sent a message, or a telephone call? They always avoided telephoning in the mornings because her husband was sure to be in his study till twelve, and likely to emerge suddenly on the landing and unhook the receiver himself. But in any case, unless Phil decided to miss the train, there would be no time for telephoning. She was so notoriously unpunctual that till the very last minute he would be fuming up and down the platform, or leaning out watching for her; and when the train started he would start with it. Oh, she knew that as well as she knew her own name!

And how indeed could he do otherwise? The train they had fixed upon was the last which would get them to New York in time to catch the steamer – and the steamer was the only one to sail that month for Progreso. Dates and hours had been fitted together with the boyish nicety which characterised Phil when he was dealing with anything connected with his travels. Bent above maps and time-tables, his face grew as round and absorbed as a schoolboy's. And in New York, she knew, there would be just time to pick up his outfit: he'd talked to her enough about that famous outfit! Just time for that, and a taxi-rush to the steamer. And the expedition came first in his mind – that fact had always been clear to Nalda. It was as it should be;

as she wanted it to be. . . And if a poor little woman, who had imagined she couldn't live without him, got cold feet at the last minute, and failed to turn up – well, with the exploring fever on him, he'd probably take even that with a shrug, for he was committed to the enterprise, and would have to go without her if she failed him.

And she *had* failed him – through sheer muddle-headedness, through unpardonable stupidity, the childish blunder of mistaking one day of the week for another, she had failed him; and of course he would always think it was because she hadn't had the pluck. . .

'You'll see, my child, you'll funk it at the last minute. No woman really likes hardships; and this trip isn't going to be any season at Palm Beach,' Phil had warned her, laughing and throwing out his chest a little.

She found herself on her own door-step, and fumbled for her latch-key. It was not in her bag, and she rang the bell furiously.

'Is there a telegram?'

No; the maid who opened the door said there was none. Of course there was none; how should there be?

'I've mislaid my key,' Nalda said, to say something.

The maid smiled. 'Here it is. The Professor picked it up on the door-step.'

Of course – how like her again! Lucky she hadn't dropped the passport and the travellers' cheques while she was about it.

She started up the stairs to her room. She thought: 'If I hadn't mistaken the day I should have gone up these stairs tonight for the last time. I should never again have noticed that tear in the carpet, and said to myself: 'I must telephone at once to the upholsterer to send somebody to mend it'.'

Time and again her husband had said to her: 'For heaven's sake get that tear in the stair-carpet mended. It'll be the death of somebody. I caught my heel in it again last night.' She had always said yes, and then forgotten; and it was because she had that kind of mind, with great holes in it like the hole in the stair-carpet, that, instead of going up those stairs for the last time tonight, she would probably continue to go up them every day for the rest of her life. It was queer, how unexpected things hung together...

As she mounted the stairs her mind continued to rush through every possibility of retrieving the blunder of the date. But already she had the feeling that these dizzy feats of readjustment were being performed in the void, by some one who was not really herself. No; her real self was here, on this shabby familiar stair-carpet, going up to the room which had been the setting of her monotonous married years. It was curious; she had no faith any longer in the reality of that other future toward which, a few hours ago, every drop of blood in her was straining. What if she should rush out again, and at least send off a wire to the steamer? No; that was not possible either. The steamer sailed at seven, and her bedroom clock (which always kept good time because Vincent saw to the clocks) told her that it was already past the hour.

But would she have telegraphed, even if there had been time? What could she have said? 'Made a mistake in the day'? That was too humiliating... Better let him think that her courage *had* failed her ... or that a sense of duty... But no; not that either. They had made too many jokes about that coward's pretext, the Sense of Duty...

She tossed off her hat and sat down wearily. Her mind, sick of revolving in its endless maze, became suddenly cold and quiescent. This was the way things had been meant to happen, she supposed...

Well, she thought, at any rate she would be alone this one evening. Thursday – the first Thursday of the month – was the night of her husband's Club dinner; the dinner which was the cause of so many pleasantries, and so much secret anxiety, among the ladies of the Faculty, because of the late hour at which their husbands got home from it, but which had never troubled Nalda, since at eleven she could always count on hearing Vincent's punctual key in the lock.

Poor old Vincent –! She wondered what he would have said and done, if, returning home, he had found her gone?

There was a knock on the door and she started up. A telegram after all? 'Yes?' she said.

'Dinner's ready, ma'am. The Professor sent me up to say –'

'Dinner?' She repeated the word slowly, trying to fit it into her mind. 'I don't want any dinner. Mr. Craig's going out, isn't he?'

'Why, no; he hasn't mentioned it.'

She stared at the woman, bewildered. It was extraordinary, incredible! Her husband, who never forgot anything, whose memory was so irritatingly retentive of every trifle, her husband had actually forgotten his famous Club dinner, the one social event which seemed to give him any pleasure, the one non-professional engagement with which nothing was allowed to interfere.

'Are you sure Mr. Craig hasn't gone out?'

'No, ma'am; Mr. Craig's in the library.'

'But it's the night of his Club dinner. He must have forgotten. . . I'll go down.'

She sprang up, and then stood still, hesitating. She had been so thankful that she would not have to see her husband that night. What could have happened? Perhaps he had simply fallen asleep before the library fire. Daytime naps were not his habit – but she knew he had been very much overworked of late, and had reached a difficult controversial point in the course of lectures he was preparing. Even Winna Norman, who seldom noticed anything beyond the range of her personal interests, had said not long ago: 'Look here, what's the matter with your domestic jailer? Looks as if he's been dug up. You'd better pack him off somewhere for a change.'

Nalda had not paid any heed at the moment; she had no time to study Vincent's features, and she had fancied that Winna, who liked stirring up mud, and certainly suspected something about herself and Phil Ingerson, had simply wanted to give her a fright – or perhaps a warning. Fright or warning, Nalda had taken neither; she was too securely encased in her own bliss. But now she did remember being conscious that her husband of late had looked suddenly older, walked with a stoop. . . She went slowly down the stairs, and slowly turned the handle of the library door.

'Vincent –?'

He was not asleep now, at any rate. He stood up quickly, and faced her with his dry smile. 'Late, eh – as usual?' (Oh, why had he hit on that hated phrase?) 'I'm rather disposed to dine, if you've no objection.'

'But you're dining out tonight! Have you forgotten?' Even through the thick cloud of her misery it gave her a passing gleam of satisfaction to remind him, for once, of something he had forgotten.

His face clouded. 'Dining out? Again? Good heavens! You promised solemnly only last week that you wouldn't accept another invitation for me till I'd finished this job. . .'

'I haven't. Tonight is your Club dinner.'

'Club dinner?' He looked relieved. 'You're a day out, my child. My Club dinner's tomorrow.'

'It always has been on a Thursday.'

'Well – tomorrow's Thursday.'

She gave a little nervous laugh. 'No; today is.'

'Today Thursday?' He smiled again. 'I sometimes wonder how you ever keep your own engagements, let alone trying to keep mine for me.'

'But this is Thursday – it *is* Thursday,' she repeated vehemently, as though, after what she had undergone, it *had* to be Thursday now, for all time, if she said so.

'Bless your innocent heart, today's Wednesday.'

'Wednesday?'

'Certainly. Why – what's wrong? Does it interfere with your plans, its being Wednesday?'

She stood before him, conscious that she was beginning to tremble. What on earth did his question mean? She clutched blindly at the back of the nearest chair. 'With my plans?'

'I thought maybe you'd arranged to run round to Winna Norman's and talk about clothes,' he joked.

She gave another little laugh, this time of relief; then she checked herself fiercely, as she felt the dangerous ripple prolonging itself in her throat. 'It *is* Thursday, you know,' she insisted with dry lips.

He lifted the calendar from his desk and held it out to her. 'I turn it myself every morning. I don't trust anybody else to do it for me,' he said, strangely echoing the hair-dresser's words. She read: WEDNESDAY, in great staring block letters, and suddenly the uncontrollable ripple rose in her throat and forced its way through her clenched lips. She dropped down into the chair on which she had been leaning, and laughed and laughed and laughed. . .

The last she remembered was seeing her husband's face above her, gray with fright, and saying to herself: 'Winna was right. . . Poor old Vincent – he looks like death. I'll have to take him away somewhere. . .'

Then she knew that his arms were about her, and felt that with painful precautions he was lowering her slowly to the sofa, pushing back her suffocating hair, composing her limbs as if, with pious hands, he were preparing her for her final rest. . .

'Poor old Vincent,' she murmured again, as the fog closed in on her.

CONFESSION

I

This is the way it began; stupidly, trivially, out of nothing, as fatal things do.

I was sitting at the corner table in the hotel restaurant; I mean the left-hand corner as you enter from the hall. . . As if that mattered! A table in that angle, with a view over the mountains, was too good for an unaccompanied traveller, and I had it only because the head-waiter was a good-natured fellow who . . . As if that mattered, either! Why can't I come to the point?

The point is that, entering the restaurant that day with the doubtful step of the newly-arrived, she was given the table next to me. Colossal Event – eh? But if you've ever known what it is, after a winter of semi-invalidism on the Nile, to be told that, before you're fit to go back and take up your job in New York – before that little leak in your lung is patched up tight – you've got to undergo another three or four months of convalescence on top of an Alp; if you've dragged through all those stages of recovery, first among one pack of hotel idlers, then among another, you'll know what small incidents can become Colossal Events against the empty horizon of your idleness.

Not that a New York banker's office (even before the depression) commanded a very wide horizon, as I understand horizons; but before arguing that point with me, wait and see what it's like to look out day after day on a dead-level of inoccupation, and you'll know what a towering affair it may become to have your temperature go up a point, or a woman you haven't seen before stroll into the dining-room, and sit down at the table next to yours.

But what magnified this very ordinary incident for me was the immediate sense of something out of the ordinary in the woman herself. Beauty? No; not even. (I say 'even' because there are far deadlier weapons, as we all know.) No, she was not beautiful; she was not particularly young; and though she carried herself well, and was well dressed (though over-expensively, I thought), there was nothing in that to single her out in a fashionable crowd.

What then? Well, what struck me first in her was a shy but intense curiosity about everything in that assemblage of commonplace and shop-worn people. Here was a woman, evidently well-bred and well-off, to whom a fashionable hotel restaurant in the En-gadine during the summer was apparently a sight so unusual, and composed of elements so novel and inexplicable, that she could hardly remember to eat in the subdued excitement of watching all that was going on about her.

As to her own appearance, it obviously did not preoccupy her – or figured only as an element of her general and rather graceful timidity. She was so busy observing all the dull commonplace people about her that it had presumably never occurred to her that she, who was neither dull nor commonplace, might be herself the subject of observation. (Already I found myself resenting any too protracted stare from the other tables.)

Well, to come down to particulars: she was middling tall, slight, almost thin; pale, with a long somewhat narrow face and dark hair; and her wide blue-gray eyes were so light and clear that her hair and complexion seemed dusky in contrast. A melancholy mouth, which lit up suddenly when she smiled – but her smiles were rare. Dress, sober, costly, severely 'lady-like'; her whole appearance, shall I say a trifle old-fashioned – or perhaps merely provincial? But certainly it was not only her dress which singled her out from the standardised beauties at the other tables. Perhaps it was the fact that her air of social inexperience was combined with a look, about the mouth and eyes, of having had more experience, of some other sort, than any woman in the room.

But of what sort? That was what baffled me. I could only sum it up by saying to myself that she was different; which, of course, is what every man feels about the woman he is about to fall in love with, no matter how painfully usual she may appear to others. But I had no idea that I was going to fall in love with the lady at the next table, and when I defined her as 'different' I did not mean it subjectively, did not mean different to *me*, but in herself, mysteriously, and independently of the particular impression she made on me. In short, she appeared, in spite of her dress and bearing, to be a little uncertain and ill at ease in the ordinary social scene, but at home and sure of herself elsewhere. Where?

I was still asking myself this when she was joined by a companion. One of the things one learns in travelling is to find out about people by studying their associates; and I wished that the lady who interested me had not furnished me with this particular kind of clue. The woman who joined her was probably of about her own age; but that seemed to be the only point of resemblance between them. The newcomer was stout, with mahogany-dyed hair, and small eyes set too close to a coarse nose. Her complexion, through a careless powdering, was flushed, and netted with little red veins, and her chin sloped back under a vulgar mouth to a heavy white throat. I had hoped she was only a chance acquaintance of the dark lady's; but she took her seat without speaking, and began to study the menu without as much as a glance at her companion. They were fellow-travellers, then; and though the newcomer was as richly dressed as the other, and I judged more fashionably, I detected at once that she was a subordinate, probably a paid one, and that she sought to conceal it by an exaggerated assumption of equality. But how could the one woman have chosen the other as a companion? It disturbed my mental picture of the dark lady to have to fit into it what was evidently no chance association.

'Have you ordered my beer?' the last comer asked, drawing off her long gloves from thick red fingers crammed with rings (the dark lady wore none, I had noticed.)

'No, I haven't,' said the other.

Her tone somehow suggested: 'Why should I? Can't you ask for what you want yourself?' But a moment later she had signed to the head-waiter, and said, in a low tone: 'Miss Wilpert's Pilsener, please – as usual.'

'Yes; *as usual.* Only nobody ever remembers it! I used to be a lot better served when I had to wait on myself.'

The dark lady gave a faint laugh of protest.

Miss Wilpert, after a critical glance at the dish presented to her, transferred a copious portion to her plate, and squared herself before it. I could almost imagine a napkin tucked into the neck of her dress, below the crease in her heavy white throat.

'There were three women ahead of me at the hairdresser's,' she grumbled.

The dark lady glanced at her absently. 'It doesn't matter.'

'What doesn't matter?' snapped her companion. 'That I should be kept there two hours, and have to wait till two o'clock for my lunch?'

'I meant that your being late didn't matter to me.'

'I daresay not,' retorted Miss Wilpert. She poured down a draught of Pilsener, and set the empty glass beside her plate. 'So you're in the 'nothing matters' mood again, are you?' she said, looking critically at her companion.

The latter smiled faintly. 'Yes.'

'Well, then – what are we staying here for? You needn't sacrifice yourself for me, you know.'

A lady, finishing her lunch, crossed the room, and in passing out stopped to speak to my neighbour. 'Oh, Mrs. Ingram' (so her name was Ingram), 'can't we persuade you to join us at bridge when you've had your coffee?'

Mrs. Ingram smiled, but shook her head. 'Thank you so much. But you know I don't play cards.'

'Principles!' jerked out Miss Wilpert, wiping her rouged lips after a second glass of Pilsener. She waved her fat hand toward the retreating lady. 'I'll join up with you in half an hour,' she cried in a penetrating tone.

'Oh, do,' said the lady with an indifferent nod.

I had finished my lunch, drunk my coffee, and smoked more than my strict ration of cigarettes. There was no other excuse for lingering, and I got up and walked out of the restaurant. My friend Antoine, the head-waiter, was standing near the door, and in passing I let my lips shape the inaudible question: 'The lady at the next table?'

Antoine knew every one, and also every one's history. I wondered why he hesitated for a moment before replying: 'Ah – Mrs. Ingram? Yes. From California.'

'Er – regular visitor?'

'No. I think on her first trip to Europe.'

'Ah. Then the other lady's showing her about?'

Antoine gave a shrug. 'I think not. She seems also new.'

'I like the table you've given me, Antoine,' I remarked; and he nodded compliantly.

I was surprised, therefore, that when I came down to dinner that evening I had been assigned to another seat, on the farther side of the restaurant. I asked for Antoine, but it was his evening off, and the understudy who replaced him could only say that I had been moved by Antoine's express orders. 'Perhaps it was on account of the draught, sir.'

'Draught be blowed! Can't I be given back my table?'

He was very sorry, but, as I could see, the table had been allotted to an infirm old lady, whom it would be difficult, and indeed impossible, to disturb.

'Very well, then. At lunch tomorrow I shall expect to have it back,' I said severely.

In looking back over the convalescent life, it is hard to recall the exaggerated importance every trifle assumes when there are only trifles to occupy one. I was furious at having had my place changed; and still more so when, the next day at lunch, Antoine, as a matter of course, conducted me to the table I had indignantly rejected the night before.

'What does this mean? I told you I wanted to go back to that corner table –'

Not a muscle moved in his non-committal yet all-communicating face. 'So sorry, sir.'

'Sorry? Why, you promised me –'

'What can I do? Those ladies have our most expensive suite; and they're here for the season.'

'Well, what's the matter with the ladies? I've no objection to them. They're my compatriots.'

Antoine gave me a spectral smile. 'That appears to be the reason, sir.'

'The reason? They've given you a reason for asking to have me moved?'

'The big red one did. The other, Mrs. Ingram, as you can see, is quite different – though both are a little odd,' he added thoughtfully.

'Well – the big red one?'

'The *dame de compagnie*. You must excuse me, sir; but she says she doesn't like Americans. And as the management are anxious to oblige Mrs. Ingram –'

I gave a haughty laugh. 'I see. Whereas a humble lodger like myself – But there are other hotels at Mont Soleil, you may remind the management from me.'

'Oh, Monsieur, Monsieur – you can't be so severe on a lady's whim,' Antoine murmured reprovingly.

Of course I couldn't. Antoine's advice was always educational. I shrugged, and accepting my banishment, looked about for another interesting neighbour to watch instead of Mrs. Ingram. But I found that no one else interested me. . .

II

'Don't you think you might tell me now,' I said to Mrs. Ingram a few days later, 'why your friend insisted on banishing me to the farther end of the restaurant?'

I need hardly say that, in spite of Miss Wilpert's prejudice against her compatriots, she had not been able to prevent my making the acquaintance of Mrs. Ingram. I forget how it came about – the pretext of a dropped letter, a deck chair to be moved out of the sun, or one of the hundred devices which bring two people together when they are living idle lives under the same roof. I had not gained my end without difficulty, however, for the ill-assorted pair were almost always together. But luckily Miss Wilpert played bridge, and Mrs. Ingram did not, and before long I had learned to profit by this opportunity, and in the course of time to make the fullest use of it.

Yet after a fortnight I had to own that I did not know much more about Mrs. Ingram than when I had first seen her. She was younger than I had thought, probably not over thirty-two or three; she was wealthy; she was shy; she came from California, or at any rate had lived there. For the last two years or more she appeared to have travelled, encircling the globe, and making long stays in places as far apart as Ceylon, Teneriffe, Rio and Cairo. She seemed, on the whole, to have enjoyed these wanderings. She asked me many questions about the countries she had visited, and I saw that she belonged to the class of intelligent but untaught travellers who can learn more by verbal explanations than from books. Unprepared as she was for the sights awaiting her, she had necessarily observed little, and understood less; but she had been struck by the more conspicuous features of the journey, and the Taj, the Parthenon and the Pyramids had not escaped her. On the subject of her travels she was at least superficially communicative; and as she never alluded to husband or child, or to any other friend or relative, I was driven to conclude that Miss Wilpert had been her only companion. This deepened the mystery, and made me feel that I knew no more of her real self than on the day when I had first seen her; but, perhaps partly for that reason, I found her increasingly interesting. It was clear that she shrank from strangers, but I could not help seeing that with me she was happy and at ease, and as ready as I was to profit by our opportunities of being together. It was only when Miss Wilpert appeared that her old shyness returned, and I suspected that she was reluctant to let her companion see what good friends we had become.

I had put my indiscreet question about Miss Wilpert somewhat abruptly, in the hope of startling Mrs. Ingram out of her usual reserve; and I saw by the quick rise of colour under her pale skin that I had nearly succeeded. But after a moment she replied, with a smile: 'I can't believe Cassie ever said anything so silly.'

'You can't? Then I wish you'd ask her; and if it was just an invention of that head-waiter's I'll make him give me back my table before he's a day older.'

Mrs. Ingram still smiled. 'I hope you won't make a fuss about such a trifle. Perhaps Cassie did say something foolish. She's not used to travelling, and sometimes takes odd notions.'

The ambiguity of the answer was obviously meant to warn me off; but having risked one question I was determined to risk another. 'Miss Wilpert's a very old friend, I suppose?'

'Yes; very,' said Mrs. Ingram non-committally.

'And was she always with you when you were at home?'

My question seemed to find her unprepared. 'At home –?'

'I mean, where you lived. California, wasn't it?'

She looked relieved. 'Oh, yes; Cassie Wilpert was with me in California.'

'But there she must have had to associate with her compatriots?'

'Yes; that's one reason why she was so glad when I decided to travel,' said Mrs. Ingram with a faint touch of irony, and then added: 'Poor Cassie was very unhappy at one time; there were people who were unkind to her. That accounts for her prejudices, I suppose.'

'I'm sorry I'm one of them. What can I do to make up to her?'

I fancied I saw a slight look of alarm in Mrs. Ingram's eyes. 'Oh, you'd much better leave her alone.'

'But she's always with you; and I don't want to leave you alone.'

Mrs. Ingram smiled, and then sighed. 'We shall be going soon now.'

'And then Miss Wilpert will be rid of me?'

Mrs. Ingram looked at me quickly; her eyes were plaintive, almost entreating. 'I shall never leave her; she's been like a – a sister to me,' she murmured, answering a question I had not put.

The word startled me; and I noticed that Mrs. Ingram had hesitated a moment before pronouncing it. A sister to her – that coarse red-handed woman? The words sounded as if they had been spoken by rote. I saw at once that they did not express the speaker's real feeling, and that, whatever that was, she did not mean to let me find it out.

Some of the bridge-players with whom Miss Wilpert consorted were coming toward us, and I stood up to leave. 'Don't let Miss Wilpert carry you off on my account. I promise you I'll keep out of her way,' I said, laughing.

Mrs. Ingram straightened herself almost imperiously. 'I'm not at Miss Wilpert's orders; she can't take me away from any place I choose to stay in,' she said; but a moment later, lowering her voice, she breathed to me quickly: 'Go now; I see her coming.'

III

I don't mind telling you that I was not altogether happy about my attitude toward Mrs. Ingram. I'm not given to prying into other people's secrets; yet I had not scrupled to try to trap her into revealing hers. For that there was a secret I was now convinced; and I excused myself for trying to get to the bottom of it by the fact that I was sure I should find Miss Wilpert there, and that the idea was abhorrent to me. The relation between the two women, I had by now discovered, was one of mutual animosity; not the kind of animosity which may be the disguise of more complicated sentiments, but the simple incompatibility that was bound to exist between two women so different in class and character. Miss Wilpert was a coarse, uneducated woman, with, as far as I could see, no redeeming qualities, moral or mental, to bridge the distance between herself and her companion; and the mystery was that any past tie or obligation, however strong, should have made Mrs. Ingram tolerate her.

I knew how easily rich and idle women may become dependent on some vulgar tyrannical housekeeper or companion who renders them services and saves them trouble; but I saw at once that this theory did not explain the situation. On the contrary, it was Miss Wilpert who was dependent on Mrs. Ingram, who looked to her as guide, interpreter, and manager of their strange association. Miss Wilpert possessed no language but her own, and of that only a local vernacular which made it difficult to explain her wants (and they were many) even to the polyglot servants of a Swiss hotel. Mrs. Ingram spoke a carefully acquired if laborious French, and was conscientiously preparing for a winter in Naples by taking a daily lesson in Italian; and I noticed that whenever an order was to be given, an excursion planned, or any slight change effected in the day's arrangements, Miss Wilpert, suddenly embarrassed and helpless, always waited for Mrs. Ingram to interpret for her. It was obvious, therefore, that she was a burden and not a help to her employer, and that I must look deeper to discover the nature of their bond.

Mrs. Ingram, guide-book in hand, appealed to me one day about their autumn plans. 'I think we shall be leaving next week; and they say here we ought not to miss the Italian lakes.'

'Leaving next week? But why? The lakes are not at their best till after the middle of September. You'll find them very stuffy after this high air.'

Mrs. Ingram sighed. 'Cassie's tired of it here. She says she doesn't like the people.'

I looked at her, and then ventured with a smile: 'Don't you mean that she doesn't like me?'

'I don't see why you think that –'

'Well, I daresay it sounds rather fatuous. But you *do* know why I think it; and you think it yourself.' I hesitated a moment, and then went on, lowering my voice: 'Since you attach such importance to Miss Wilpert's opinions, it's natural I should want to know why she dislikes seeing me with you.'

Mrs. Ingram looked at me helplessly. 'Well, if she doesn't like you –'

'Yes; but in reality I don't think it's me she dislikes, but the fact of my being with you.'

She looked disturbed at this. 'But if she dislikes you, it's natural she shouldn't want you to be with me.'

'And do her likes and dislikes regulate all your friendships?'

'Friendships? I've so few; I know hardly any one,' said Mrs. Ingram, looking away.

'You'd have as many as you chose if she'd let you,' I broke out angrily.

She drew herself up with the air of dignity she could assume on occasion. 'I don't know why you find so much pleasure in saying disagreeable things to me about my – my friend.'

The answer rushed to my lips: 'Why did she begin by saying disagreeable things about me?' – but just in time I saw that I was on the brink of a futile wrangle with the woman whom, at that moment, I was the most anxious not to displease. How anxious, indeed, I now saw for the first time, in the light of my own anger. For what on earth did I care for the disapproval of a creature like Miss Wilpert, except as it interfered with my growing wish to stand well with Kate Ingram? The answer I did make sprang to my lips before I could repress it. 'Because – you must know by this time. Because I can't bear that anything or any one should come between us.'

'Between us –?'

I pressed on, hardly knowing what I was saying. 'Because nothing matters to me as much as what you feel about me. In fact, nothing else matters at all.'

The words had rushed out, lighting up the depths of my feeling as much to myself as to Mrs. Ingram. Only then did I remember how little I knew of the woman to whom they were addressed – not even her maiden name, nor as much as one fact of her past history. I did not even know if she were married, widowed or divorced. All I did know was that I had fallen in love with her – and had told her so.

She sat motionless, without a word. But suddenly her eyes filled, and I saw that her lips were trembling too much for her to speak.

'Kate –' I entreated; but she drew back, shaking her head.

'No –'

'Why 'no'? Because I've made you angry –?'

She shook her head again. 'I feel that you're a true friend –'

'I want you to feel much more than that.'

'It's all I can ever feel – for any one. I shall never – never . . .' She broke down, and sat struggling with her tears.

'Do you say that because you're not free?'

'Oh, no – oh, no –'

'Then is it because you don't like me? Tell me that, and I won't trouble you again.'

We were sitting alone in a deserted corner of the lounge. The diners had scattered to the wide verandahs, the card-room or the bar. Miss Wilpert was safely engaged with a party of bridge-players in the farthest room of the suite, and I had imagined that at last I should be able to have my talk out with Mrs. Ingram. I had hardly meant it to take so grave a turn; but now that I had spoken I knew my choice was made.

'If you tell me you don't like me, I won't trouble you any more,' I repeated, trying to keep her eyes on mine. Her lids quivered, and she looked down at her uneasy hands. I had often noticed that her hands were the only unquiet things about her, and now she sat clasping and unclasping them without ceasing.

'I can't tell you that I don't like you,' she said, very low. I leaned over to capture those restless fingers, and quiet them in mine; but at the same moment she gave a start, and I saw that she was not looking at me, but over my shoulder at some one who must have crossed the lounge behind me. I turned and saw a man I had not noticed before in the hotel, but whose short square-shouldered figure struck me as vaguely familiar.

'Is that some one you know?' I asked, surprised by the look in her face.

'N-no. I thought it was. . . I must have been mistaken. . .' I saw that she was struggling to recover her self-control, and I looked again at the newcomer, who had stopped on his way to the bar to speak to one of the hall-porters.

'Why, I believe it's Jimmy Shreve – Shreve of the New York *Evening Star*,' I said. 'It looks like him. Do you know him?'

'No.'

'Then, please – won't you answer the question I was just asking you?'

She had grown very pale, and was twisting her long fingers distressfully. 'Oh, not now; not now. . .'

'Why not now? After what you've told me, do you suppose I'm going to be put off without a reason?'

'There's my reason!' she exclaimed with a nervous laugh. I looked around, and saw Miss Wilpert approaching. She looked unusually large and flushed, and her elaborate evening dress showed a displeasing expanse of too-white skin.

'Ah, that's your reason? I thought so!' I broke out bitterly.

One of Mrs. Ingram's quick blushes overswept her. 'I didn't mean that – you've no right to say so. I only meant that I'd promised to go with her. . .'

Miss Wilpert was already towering over us, loud-breathing and crimson. I suspected that in the intervals of bridge she had more than once sought refreshment at the bar. 'Well, so this is where you've hidden yourself away, is it? I've hunted for you all over the place; but I didn't suppose you'd choose a dark corner under the stairs. I presume you've forgotten that you asked them to reserve seats for us for those Javanese dances. They won't keep our places much longer; the ball-room's packed already.'

I sat still, almost holding my breath, and watched the two women. I guessed that a crucial point in the struggle between them had been reached, and that a word from me might wreck my chances. Mrs. Ingram's colour faded quickly, as it always did, but she forced a nervous smile. 'I'd no idea it was so late.'

'Well, if your watch has stopped, there's the hall clock right in front of you,' said Miss Wilpert, with quick panting breaths between the words. She waited a moment. 'Are you coming?'

Mrs. Ingram leaned back in her deep armchair. 'Well, no – I don't believe I am.'

'You're *not*?'

'No. I think I like it better here.'

'But you must be crazy! You asked that Italian Countess to keep us two seats next to hers –'

'Well, you can go and ask her to excuse me – say I'm tired. The ball-room's always so hot.'

'Land's sake! How'm I going to tell her all that in Italian? You know she don't speak a word of English. She'll think it's pretty funny if you don't come; and so will the others. You always say you hate to have people talk about you; and yet here you sit, stowed away in this dark corner, like a school-girl with her boy friend at a Commencement dance –'

Mrs. Ingram stood up quickly. 'Cassie, I'm afraid you must have been losing at bridge. I never heard you talk so foolishly. But of course I'll come if you think the Countess expects us.' She turned to me with a little smile, and suddenly, shyly, held out her hand. 'You'll tell me the rest tomorrow morning,' she said, looking straight at me for an instant; then she turned and followed Cassie Wilpert.

I stood watching them with a thumping heart. I didn't know what held these women together, but I felt that in the last few minutes a link of the chain between them had been loosened, and I could hardly wait to see it snap.

I was still standing there when the man who had attracted Mrs. Ingram's notice came out of the bar, and walked toward me; and I saw that it was in fact my old acquaintance Jimmy Shreve, the bright particular ornament of the *Evening Star*. We had not met for a year or more, and his surprise at the encounter was as great as mine. 'Funny, coming across you in this jazz crowd. I'm here to get away from my newspaper; but what has brought you?'

I explained that I had been ill the previous year, and, by the doctor's orders, was working out in the Alps the last months of my convalescence; and he listened with the absent-minded sympathy which one's friends give to one's ailments, particularly when they are on the mend.

'Well – well – too bad you've had such a mean time. Glad you're out of it now, anyway,' he muttered, snapping a reluctant cigarette-lighter, and finally having recourse to mine. As he bent over it he said suddenly: 'Well, what about Kate Spain?'

I looked at him in bewilderment. For a moment the question was so unintelligible that I wondered if he too were a sufferer, and had been sent to the heights for medical reasons; but his sharp little professional eyes burned with a steady spark of curiosity as he took a close-up of me across the lighter. And then I understood; at least I understood the allusion, though its relevance escaped me.

'Kate Spain? Oh, you mean that murder trial at Cayuga? You got me a card for it, didn't you? But I wasn't able to go.'

'I remember. But you've made up for it since, I see.' He continued to twinkle at me meaningly; but I was still groping. 'What do you think of her?' he repeated.

'Think of her? Why on earth should I think of her at all?'

He drew back and squared his sturdy shoulders in evident enjoyment. 'Why, because you've been talking to her as hard as you could for the last two hours,' he chuckled.

I stood looking at him blankly. Again it occurred to me that under his tight journalistic mask something had loosened and gone adrift. But I looked at the steadiness of the stumpy fingers which held his cigarette. The man had himself under perfect control.

'Kate Spain?' I said, collecting myself. 'Does that lady I was talking to really look to you like a murderess?'

Shreve made a dubious gesture. 'I'm not so sure what murderesses look like. But, as it happens, Kate Spain was acquitted.'

'So she was. Still, I don't think I'll tell Mrs. Ingram that she looks like her.'

Shreve smiled incredulously. 'Mrs. Ingram? Is that what you call her?'

'It's her name. I was with Mrs. Ingram, of California.'

'No, you weren't. You were with Kate Spain. She knows me well enough – ask her. I met her face to face just now, going into the ball-room. She was with a red-headed Jezebel that I don't know.'

'Ah, you don't know the red-headed lady? Well, that shows you're mistaken. For Miss Cassie Wilpert has lived with

Mrs. Ingram as her companion for several years. They're inseparable.'

Shreve tossed away his cigarette and stood staring at me. 'Cassie Wilpert? Is that what that great dressed-up prize-fighter with all the jewelry calls herself? Why, see here, Severance, Cassie was the servant girl's name, sure enough: Cassie – don't you remember? It was her evidence that got Kate Spain off. But at the trial she was a thin haggard Irish girl in dirty calico. To be sure, I suppose old Ezra Spain starved his servant as thoroughly as he starved his daughter. You remember Cassie's description of the daily fare: Sunday, boiled mutton; Monday, cold mutton; Tuesday, mutton hash; Wednesday, mutton stew – and I forget what day the dog got the mutton bone. Why, it was Cassie who knocked the prosecution all to pieces. At first it was doubtful how the case would go; but she testified that she and Kate Spain were out shopping together when the old man was murdered; and the prosecution was never able to shake her evidence.'

Remember it? Of course I remembered every detail of it, with a precision which startled me, considering I had never, to my knowledge, given the Kate Spain trial a thought since the talk about it had died out with the woman's acquittal. Now it all came back to me, every scrap of evidence, all the sordid and sinister gossip let loose by the trial: the tale of Ezra Spain, the wealthy miser and tyrant, of whom no one in his native town had a good word to say, who was reported to have let his wife die of neglect because he would not send for a doctor till it was too late, and who had been too mean to supply her with food and medicines, or to provide a trained nurse for her. After his wife's death his daughter had continued to live with him, brow-beaten and starved in her turn, and apparently lacking the courage to cast herself penniless and inexperienced upon the world. It had been almost with a sense of relief that Cayuga had learned of the old man's murder by a wandering tramp who had found him alone in the house, and had killed him in his sleep, and got away with what little money there was. Now at last, people said, that poor persecuted daughter with the wistful eyes and the frightened smile would be free, would be rich, would be able to come out of her prison, and marry and enjoy her life, instead of wasting and dying as her mother had died. And then came the incredible rumour that, instead of coming out of prison – the prison of her father's house – she was to go into another, the kind one entered in hand-cuffs, between two jailers: was to go there accused of her father's murder.

'I've got it now! Cassie Donovan – that was the servant's name,' Shreve suddenly exclaimed. 'Don't you remember?'

'No, I don't. But this woman's name, as I've told you, isn't Donovan – it's Wilpert, Miss Wilpert.'

'Her new name, you mean? Yes. And Kate Spain's new name, you say, is Mrs. Ingram. Can't you see that the first thing they'd do, when they left Cayuga, would be to change their names?'

'Why should they, when nothing was proved against them? And you say yourself you didn't recognise Miss Wilpert,' I insisted, struggling to maintain my incredulity.

'No; I didn't remember that she might have got fat and dyed her hair. I guess they do themselves like fighting cocks now, to make up for past privations. They say the old man cut up even fatter than people expected. But prosperity hasn't changed Kate Spain. I knew her at once; I'd have known her anywhere. And she knew me.'

'She didn't know you,' I broke out; 'she said she was mistaken.'

Shreve pounced on this in a flash. 'Ah – so at first she thought she did?' He laughed. 'I don't wonder she said afterward she was mistaken. I don't dye my hair yet, but I'm afraid I've put on nearly as much weight as Cassie Donovan.' He paused again, and then added: 'All the same, Severance, she did know me.'

I looked at the little journalist and laughed back at him.

'What are you laughing at?'

'At you. At such a perfect case of professional deformation. Wherever you go you're bound to spot a criminal; but I should have thought even Mont Soleil could have produced a likelier specimen than my friend Mrs. Ingram.'

He looked a little startled at my tone. 'Oh, see here; if she's such a friend I'm sorry I said anything.'

I rose to heights of tolerance. 'Nothing you can say can harm her, my dear fellow.'

'Harm her? Why on earth should it? I don't want to harm her.'

'Then don't go about spreading such ridiculous gossip. I don't suppose any one cares to be mistaken for a woman who's been tried for her life; and if I were a relation of Mrs. Ingram's I'm bound to tell you I should feel obliged to put a stop to your talk.'

He stared in surprise, and I thought he was going to retort in the same tone; but he was a fair-minded little fellow, and after a moment I could see he'd understood. 'All right, Severance; of course I don't want to do anything that'll bother her. . .'

'Then don't go on talking as if you still thought she was Kate Spain.'

He gave a hopeless shrug. 'All right. I won't. Only she *is*, you know; what'll you bet on it, old man?'

'Good night,' I said with a nod, and turned away. It was obviously a fixed idea with him; and what harm could such a crank do to me, much less to a woman like Mrs. Ingram?

As I left him he called after me: 'If she ain't, who is she? Tell me that, and I'll believe you.'

I walked away without answering.

IV

I went up to bed laughing inwardly at poor Jimmy Shreve. His craving for the sensational had certainly deformed his critical faculty. How it would amuse Mrs. Ingram to hear that he had identified her with the wretched Kate Spain! Well, she should hear it; we'd laugh over it together the next day. For she had said, in bidding me goodnight: 'You'll tell me the rest in the morning.' And that meant – could only mean – that she was going to listen to me, and if she were going to listen, she must be going to answer as I wished her to. . .

Those were my thoughts as I went up to my room. They were scarcely less confident while I was undressing. I had the hope, the promise almost, of what, at the moment, I most wished for – the only thing I wished for, in fact. I was amazed at the intensity with which I wished it. From the first I had tried to explain away my passion by regarding it as the idle man's tendency to fall into sentimental traps; but I had always known that what I felt was not of that nature. This quiet woman with the wide pale eyes and melancholy mouth had taken possession of me; she seemed always to have inhabited my mind and heart; and as I lay down to sleep I tried to analyze what it was in her that made her seem already a part of me.

But as soon as my light was out I knew I was going to lie awake all night; and all sorts of unsought problems instantly crowded out my sentimental musings. I had laughed at Shreve's inept question: 'If she ain't Kate Spain, who is she?' But now an insistent voice within me echoed: Who is she? What, in short, did I know of her? Not one single fact which would have permitted me to disprove his preposterous assertion. Who was she? Was she married, unmarried, divorced, a widow? Had she children, parents, relations distant or near? Where had she lived before going to California, and when had she gone there? I knew neither her birthplace, nor her maiden name, or indeed any fact about her except the all-dominating fact of herself.

In rehearsing our many talks with the pitiless lucidity of sleeplessness I saw that she had the rare gift of being a perfect listener; the kind whose silence supplies the inaudible questions and answers most qualified to draw one on. And I had been drawn on; ridiculously, fatuously, drawn on. She was in possession of all the chief facts of my modest history. She knew who I was, where I came from, who were my friends, my family, my antecedents; she was fully informed as to my plans, my hopes, my preferences, my tastes and hobbies, I had even confided to her my passion for Brahms and for book-collecting, and my dislike for the wireless, and for one of my brothers-in-law. And in return for these confidences she had given me – what? An understanding smile, and the occasional murmur: 'Oh, do you feel that too? I've always felt it.'

Such was the actual extent of my acquaintance with Mrs. Ingram; and I perceived that, though I had laughed at Jimmy Shreve's inept assertion, I should have been utterly unable to disprove it. I did not know who Mrs. Ingram was, or even one single fact about her.

From that point to supposing that she could be Kate Spain was obviously a long way. She might be – well, let's say almost anything; but not a woman accused of murder, and acquitted only because the circumstantial evidence was insufficient to hang her. I dismissed the grotesque supposition at once; there were problems enough to keep me awake without that.

When I said that I knew nothing of Mrs. Ingram I was mistaken. I knew one fact about her; that she could put up with Cassie Wilpert. It was only a clue, but I had felt from the first that it was a vital one. What conceivable interest or obligation could make a woman like Mrs. Ingram endure such an intimacy? If I knew that, I should know all I cared to know about her; not only about her outward circumstances but her inmost self.

Hitherto, in indulging my feeling for her, I had been disposed to slip past the awkward obstacle of Cassie Wilpert; but now I was resolved to face it. I meant to ask Kate Ingram to marry me. If she refused, her private affairs were obviously no business of mine; but if she accepted I meant to have the Wilpert question out with her at once.

It seemed a long time before daylight came; and then there were more hours to be passed before I could reasonably present myself to Mrs. Ingram. But at nine I sent a line to ask when she would see me; and a few minutes later my note was returned to me by the floor-waiter.

'But this isn't an answer; it's my own note,' I exclaimed.

Yes; it was my own note. He had brought it back because the lady had already left the hotel.

'Left? Gone out, you mean?'

'No; left with all her luggage. The two ladies went an hour ago.'

In a few minutes I was dressed and had hurried down to the concierge. It was a mistake, I was sure; of course Mrs. Ingram had not left. The floor-waiter, whom I had long since classed as an idiot, had simply gone to the wrong door. But no; the concierge shook his head. It was not a mistake. Mrs. Ingram and Miss Wilpert had gone away suddenly that morning by motor. The chauffeur's orders were to take them to Italy; to Baveno or Stresa, he thought; but he wasn't sure, and the ladies had left no address. The hotel servants said they had been up all night packing. The heavy luggage was to be sent to Milan; the concierge had orders to direct it to the station. That was all the information he could give – and I thought he looked at me queerly as he gave it.

V

I did not see Jimmy Shreve again before leaving Mont Soleil that day; indeed I exercised all my ingenuity in keeping out of his way. If I were to ask any further explanations, it was of Mrs. Ingram that I meant to ask them. Either she was Kate Spain, or she was not; and either way, she was the woman to whom I had declared my love. I should have thought nothing of Shreve's insinuations if I had not recalled Mrs. Ingram's start when she first saw him. She herself had owned that she had taken him for some one she knew; but even this would not have meant much if she and her companion had not disappeared from the hotel a few hours later, without leaving a message for me, or an address with the hall-porter.

I did not for a moment suppose that this disappearance was connected with my talk of the previous evening with Mrs. Ingram. She herself had expressed the wish to prolong that talk when Miss Wilpert interrupted it; and failing that, she had spontaneously suggested that we should meet again the next morning. It would have been less painful to think that she had fled before the ardour of my wooing than before the dread of what Shreve might reveal about her; but I knew the latter reason was the more likely.

The discovery stunned me. It took me some hours to get beyond the incredible idea that this woman, whose ways were so gentle, with whose whole nature I felt myself in such delightful harmony, had stood her trial as a murderess – and the murderess of her own father. But the more I revolved this possibility the less I believed in it. There might have been other – and perhaps not very creditable – reasons for her abrupt flight; but that she should be flying because she knew that Shreve had recognised her seemed, on further thought, impossible.

Then I began to look at the question from another angle. Supposing she *were* Kate Spain? Well, her father had been assassinated by a passing tramp; so the jury had decided. Probably suspicion would never have rested on her if it had not been notorious in Cayuga that the old man was a selfish miser, who for years had made his daughter's life intolerable. To those who knew the circumstances it had seemed conceivable, seemed almost natural, that the poor creature should finally turn against him. Yet she had had no difficulty in proving her innocence;

it was clearly established that she was out of the house when the crime was committed. Her having been suspected, and tried, was simply one of those horrible blunders of which innocent persons have so often been the victims. Do what she would to live it down, her name would always remain associated with that sordid tragedy; and wasn't it natural that she should flee from any reminder of it, any suspicion that she had been recognised, and her identity proclaimed by a scandal-mongering journalist? If she were Kate Spain, the dread of having the fact made known to every one in that crowded hotel was enough to drive her out of it. But if her departure had another cause, in no way connected with Shreve's arrival, might it not have been inspired by a sudden whim of Cassie Wilpert's? Mrs. Ingram had told me that Cassie was bored and wanted to get away; and it was all too clear that, however loudly she proclaimed her independence, she always ended by obeying Miss Wilpert.

It was a melancholy alternative. Poor woman – poor woman either way, I thought. And by the time I had reached this conclusion, I was in the train which was hurrying me to Milan. Whatever happened I must see her, and hear from her own lips what she was flying from.

I hadn't much hope of running down the fugitives at Stresa or Baveno. It was not likely that they would go to either of the places they had mentioned to the concierge; but I went to both the next morning, and carried out a minute inspection of all the hotel lists. As I had foreseen, the travellers were not to be found, and I was at a loss to know where to turn next. I knew, however, that the luggage the ladies had sent to Milan was not likely to arrive till the next day, and concluded that they would probably wait for it in the neighbourhood; and suddenly I remembered that I had once advised Mrs. Ingram – who was complaining that she was growing tired of fashionable hotels – to try a little *pension* on the lake of Orta, where she would be miles away from 'palaces', and from the kind of people who frequent them.

It was not likely that she would have remembered this place; but I had put a pencil stroke beside the name in her guide-book, and that might recall it to her. Orta, at any rate, was not far off; and I decided to hire a car at Stresa, and go there before carrying on my journey.

VI

I don't suppose I shall ever get out of my eyes the memory of the public sitting-room in the *pension* at Orta. It was there that I waited for Mrs. Ingram to come down, wondering if she would, and what we should say to each other when she did.

There were three windows in a row, with clean heavily starched Nottingham lace curtains carefully draped to exclude the best part of the matchless view over lake and mountains. To make up for this privation the opposite wall was adorned with a huge oil-painting of a Swiss water-fall. In the middle of the room was a table of sham ebony, with ivory inlays, most of which had long since worked out of their grooves, and on the table the usual dusty collection of tourist magazines, fashion papers, and tattered copies of *Zion's Weekly* and the *Christian Science Monitor*.

What is the human mind made of, that mine, at such a moment, should have minutely and indelibly registered these depressing details? I even remember smiling at the thought of the impression my favourite *pension* must have made on travellers who had just moved out of the most expensive suite in the Mont Soleil Palace.

And then Mrs. Ingram came in.

My first impression was that something about her dress or the arrangement of her hair had changed her. Then I saw that two dabs of rouge had been unskilfully applied to her pale cheeks, and a cloud of powder dashed over the dark semi-circles under her eyes. She must have undergone some terrible moral strain since our parting to feel the need of such a disguise.

'I thought I should find you here,' I said.

She let me take her two hands, but at first she could not speak. Then she said, in an altered voice: 'You must have wondered –'

'Yes; I wondered.'

'It was Cassie who suddenly decided –'

'I supposed so.'

She looked at me beseechingly. 'But she was right, you know.'

'Right – about what?'

Her rouged lips began to tremble, and she drew her hands out of mine.

'Before you say anything else,' I interrupted, 'there's one thing you must let me say. I want you to marry me.'

I had not meant to bring it out so abruptly; but something in her pitiful attempt to conceal her distress had drawn me closer to her, drawn me past all doubts and distrusts, all thought of evasion or delay.

She looked at me, still without speaking, and two tears ran over her lids, and streaked the untidy powder on her cheeks.

'No – no – no!' she exclaimed, lifting her thin hand and pressing it against my lips. I drew it down and held it fast.

'Why not? You knew I was going to ask you, the day before yesterday, and when we were interrupted you promised to hear me the next morning. You yourself said: 'tomorrow morning'.'

'Yes; but I didn't know then –'

'You didn't know –?'

I was still holding her, and my eyes were fixed on hers. She gave me back my look, deeply and desperately. Then she freed herself.

'Let me go. I'm Kate Spain,' she said.

We stood facing each other without speaking. Then I gave a laugh, and answered, in a voice that sounded to me as though I were shouting: 'Well, I want to marry you, Kate Spain.'

She shrank back, her hands clasped across her breast. 'You knew already? That man told you?'

'Who – Jimmy Shreve? What does it matter if he did? Was that the reason you ran away from me?' She nodded.

'And you thought I wouldn't find you?'

'I thought you wouldn't try.'

'You thought that, having told you one day that I loved you, I'd let you go out of my life the next?'

She gave me another long look. 'You – you're generous. I'm grateful. But you can't marry Kate Spain,' she said, with a little smile like the grimace on a dying face.

I had no doubt in my own mind that I could; the first sight of her had carried that conviction home, and I answered: 'Can't I, though? That's what we'll see.

'You don't know what my life is. How would you like, wherever you went, to have some one suddenly whisper behind you: 'Look. That's Kate Spain'?'

I looked at her, and for a moment found no answer. My first impulse of passionate pity had swept me past the shock of her confession; as long as she was herself, I seemed to feel, it mattered nothing to me that she was also Kate Spain. But her last words called up a sudden vision of the life she must have led since her acquittal; the life I was asking to share with her. I recalled my helpless wrath when Shreve had told me who she was; and now I seemed to hear the ugly whisper –'Kate Spain, Kate Spain' – following us from place to place, from house to house; following my wife and me.

She took my hesitation for an answer. 'You hadn't thought of that, had you? But I think of nothing else, day and night. For three years now I've been running away from the sound of my name. I tried California first; it was at the other end of the country, and some of my mother's relations lived there. They were kind to me, everybody was kind; but wherever I went I heard my name: Kate Spain – Kate Spain! I couldn't go to church, or to the theatre, or into a shop to buy a spool of thread, without hearing it. What was the use of calling myself

Mrs. Ingram, when, wherever I went, I heard Kate Spain? The very school-children knew who I was, and rushed out to see me when I passed, I used to get letters from people who collected autographs, and wanted my signature: 'Kate Spain, you know.' And when I tried shutting myself up, people said: 'What's she afraid of? Has she got something to hide, after all?' and I saw that it made my cousins uncomfortable, and shy with me, because I couldn't lead a normal life like theirs. . . After a year I couldn't stand it, and so we came away, and went round the world. . . But wherever we go it begins again: and I know now I can never get away from it.' She broke down, and hid her face for a moment. Then she looked up at me and said: 'And so you must go away, you see.'

I continued to look at her without speaking: I wanted the full strength of my will to go out to her in my answer. 'I see, on the contrary, that I must stay.'

She gave me a startled glance. 'No – no.'

'Yes, yes. Because all you say is a nervous dream; natural enough, after what you've been through, but quite unrelated to reality. You say you've thought of nothing else, day and night; but why think of it at all – in that way? Your real name is Kate Spain. Well – what of it? Why try to disguise it? You've never done anything to disgrace it. You've suffered through it, but never been abased. If you want to get rid of it there's a much simpler way; and that is to take mine instead. But meanwhile, if people ask you if you're Kate Spain, try saying yes, you are, instead of running away from them.'

She listened with bent head and interlocked hands, and I saw a softness creep about her lips. But after I had ceased she looked up at me sadly. 'You've never been tried for your life,' she said.

The words struck to the roots of my optimism. I remembered in a flash that when I had first seen her I had thought there was a look about her mouth and eyes unlike that of any other woman I had known; as if she had had a different experience from theirs. Now I knew what that experience was: the black shadow of the criminal court, and the long lonely fight to save her neck. And I'd been trying to talk reason to a woman who'd been through that!

'My poor girl – my poor child!' I held out my arms, and she fell into them and wept out her agony. There were no more words to be said; no words could help her. Only the sense of human nearness, human pity, of a man's arms about her, and his heart against hers, could draw her out of her icy hell into the common warmth of day.

Perhaps it was the thought of that healing warmth which made me suddenly want to take her away from the Nottingham lace curtains and the Swiss waterfall. For a while we sat silent, and I held her close; then I said: 'Come out for a walk with me. There are beautiful walks close by, up through the beech-woods.'

She looked at me with a timid smile. I knew now that she would do all I told her to; but before we started out I must rid my mind of another load. 'I want to have you all to myself for the rest of the day. Where's Miss Wilpert?' I asked.

Miss Wilpert was away in Milan, she said, and would not be back till late. She had gone to see about passport visas and passages on a cruising liner which was sailing from Genoa to the Ægean in a few days. The ladies thought of taking the cruise. I made no answer, and we walked out through the *pension* garden, and mounted the path to the beech-woods.

We wandered on for a long time, saying hardly anything to each other; then we sat down on the mossy steps of one of the little pilgrimage chapels among the trees. It is a place full of sweet solitude, and gradually it laid its quieting touch on the tormented creature at my side.

As we sat there the day slipped down the sky, and we watched, through the great branches, the lake turning golden and then fading, and the moon rising above the mountains. I put my hand on hers. 'And now let's make some plans,' I said.

I saw the apprehensive look come back to her eyes. 'Plans – oh, why, today?'

'Isn't it natural that two people who've decided to live together should want to talk over their future? When are we going to be married – to begin with?'

She hesitated for a long time, clasping and unclasping her unhappy hands. She had passed the stage of resistance, and I was almost sure she would not return to it again. I waited, and at length she said, looking away from me: 'But you don't like Cassie.'

The words were a shock, though I suppose I must have expected them. On the whole, I was glad they had been spoken; I had not known how to bring the subject up, and it was better she should do it for me.

'Let's say, dear, that Cassie and I don't like each other. Isn't that nearer the truth?'

'Well, perhaps; but –'

'Well, that being so, Cassie will certainly be quite as anxious to strike out for herself as I shall be to –'

She interrupted me with a sudden exclamation, 'No, no! She'll never leave me – never.'

'Never leave you? Not when you're my wife?'

She hung her head, and began her miserable finger-weaving again. 'No; not even if she lets me –'

'Lets you –?'

'Marry you,' she said in a whisper.

I mastered her hands, and forced her to turn around to me. 'Kate – look at me; straight at me. Shall I tell you something? Your worst enemy's not Kate Spain; it's Cassie Wilpert.'

She freed herself from my hold and drew back. 'My worst enemy? Cassie – she's been my only friend!'

'At the time of the trial, yes. I understand that; I understand your boundless gratitude for the help she gave you. I think I feel about that as you'd want me to. But there are other ways of showing your gratitude than by sharing the rest of your life with her.'

She listened, drooping again. 'I've tried every other way,' she said at length, below her breath.

'What other ways?'

'Oh, everything. I'm rich you know, now,' she interrupted herself, her colour rising. 'I offered her the house at Cayuga – it's a good house; they say it's very valuable. She could have sold it if she didn't want to live there. And of course I would have continued the allowance I'm giving her – I would have doubled it. But what she wanted was to stay with me; the new life she was leading amused her. She was a poor servant-girl, you know; and she had a dreadful time when – when my father was alive. She was our only help... I suppose you read about it all ... and even then she was good to me... She dared to speak to him as I didn't... And then, at the trial... The trial lasted a whole month; and it was a month with thirty-one days... Oh, don't make me go back to it – for God's sake don't!' she burst out, sobbing.

It was impossible to carry on the discussion. All I thought of was to comfort her. I helped her to her feet, whispering to her as if she had been a frightened child, and putting my arm about her to guide her down the path. She leaned on me, pressing her arm against mine. At length she said: 'You see it can't be; I always told you it could never be.'

'I see more and more that it must be; but we won't talk about that now,' I answered.

We dined quietly in a corner of the *pension* dining-room, which was filled by a colony of British old maids and retired army officers and civil servants – all so remote from the world of the 'Ezra Spain case' that, if Shreve had been there to proclaim

Mrs. Ingram's identity, the hated syllables would have waked no echo. I pointed this out to Mrs. Ingram, and reminded her that in a few years all memory of the trial would have died out, even in her own country, and she would be able to come and go unobserved and undisturbed. She shook her head and murmured: 'Cassie doesn't think so'; but when I suggested that Miss Wilpert might have her own reasons for cultivating this illusion, she did not take up the remark, and let me turn to pleasanter topics.

After dinner it was warm enough to wander down to the shore in the moonlight, and there, sitting in the little square along the lakeside, she seemed at last to cast off her haunting torment, and abandon herself to the strange new sense of happiness and safety. But presently the church bell rang the hour, and she started up, insisting that we must get back to the *pension* before Miss Wilpert's arrival. She would be there soon now, and Mrs. Ingram did not wish her to know of my presence till the next day.

I agreed to this, but stipulated that the next morning the news of our approaching marriage should be broken to Miss Wilpert, and that as soon as possible afterward I should be told of the result. I wanted to make sure of seeing Kate the moment her talk with Miss Wilpert was over, so that I could explain away – and above all, laugh away – the inevitable threats and menaces before they grew to giants in her tormented imagination. She promised to meet me between eleven and twelve in the deserted writing-room, which we were fairly sure of having to ourselves at that hour; and from there I could take her up the hillside to have our talk out undisturbed.

VII

I did not get much sleep that night, and the next morning before the *pension* was up I went out for a short row on the lake. The exercise braced my nerves, and when I got back I was prepared to face with composure whatever further disturbances were in store, I did not think they would be as bad as they appeared to my poor friend's distracted mind, and was convinced that if I could keep a firm hold on her will the worst would soon be over. It was not much past nine, and I was just finishing the *café au lait* I had ordered on returning from my row, when there was a knock at my door. It was not the casual knock of a tired servant coming to remove a tray, but a sharp nervous rap immediately followed by a second; and, before I could answer, the door opened and Miss Wilpert appeared. She came directly in, shut the door behind her, and stood looking at me with a flushed and lowering stare. But it was a look I was fairly used to seeing when her face was turned to mine, and my first thought was one of relief. If there was a scene ahead, it was best that I should bear the brunt of it; I was not half so much afraid of Miss Wilpert as of the Miss Wilpert of Kate's imagination.

I stood up and pushed forward my only armchair. 'Do you want to see me, Miss Wilpert? Do sit down.'

My visitor ignored the suggestion. 'Want to see you? God knows I don't. . . I wish we'd never laid eyes on you, either of us,' she retorted in a thick passionate voice. If the hour had not been so early I should have suspected her of having already fortified herself for the encounter.

'Then, if you won't sit down, and don't want to see me –' I began affably; but she interrupted me.

'I don't *want* to see you; but I've got to. You don't suppose I'd be here if I didn't have something to say to you?'

'Then you'd better sit down, after all.'

She shook her head, and remained leaning in the window-jamb, one elbow propped on the sill. 'What I want to know is: what business has a dandified gentleman like you to go round worming women's secrets out of them?'

Now we were coming to the point. 'If I've laid myself open to the charge,' I said quietly, 'at least it's not because I've tried to worm out yours.'

The retort took her by surprise. Her flush darkened, and she fixed her small suspicious eyes on mine.

'*My* secrets?' she flamed out. 'What do you know about my secrets?' She pulled herself together with a nervous laugh. 'What an old fool I am! You're only trying to get out of answering my question. What I want to know is what call you have to pry into my friend's private affairs?'

I hesitated, struggling again with my anger. 'If I've pried into them, as you call it, I did so, as you probably know, only after I'd asked Mrs. Ingram to be my wife.'

Miss Wilpert's laugh became an angry whinny. 'Exactly! If indeed you didn't ask her to be your wife to get her secret out of her. She's so unsuspicious that the idea never crossed her mind till I told her what I thought of the trick you'd played on her.'

'Ah, you suggested it was a trick? And how did she take the suggestion?'

Miss Wilpert stood for a moment without speaking; then she came up to the table and brought her red fist down on it with a bang. 'I tell you she'll never marry you!' she shouted.

I was on the verge of shouting back at her; but I controlled myself, conscious that we had reached the danger-point in our struggle. I said nothing, and waited.

'Don't you hear what I say?' she challenged me.

'Yes; but I refuse to take what you say from any one but Mrs. Ingram.' My composure seemed to steady Miss Wilpert. She looked at me dubiously, and then dropped into the chair I had pushed forward. 'You mean you want her to tell you herself?'

'Yes.' I sat down also, and again waited.

Miss Wilpert drew a crumpled handkerchief across her lips. 'Well, I can get her to tell you – easy enough. She'll do anything I tell her. Only I thought you'd want to act like a gentleman, and spare her another painful scene –'

'Not if she's unwilling to spare me one.'

Miss Wilpert considered this with a puzzled stare. 'She'll tell you just what I'm telling you – you can take my word for that.'

'I don't want anybody's word but hers.'

'If you think such a lot of her I'd have thought you'd rather have gone away quietly, instead of tormenting her any more.' Still I was silent, and she pulled her chair up to the table, and stretched her thick arms across it. 'See here, Mr. Severance – now you listen to me.'

'I'm listening.'

'You know I love Kate so that I wouldn't harm a hair of her head,' she whimpered. I made no comment, and she went on, in a voice grown oddly low and unsteady: 'But I don't want to quarrel with you. What's the use?'

'None whatever. I'm glad you realise it.'

'Well, then, let's you and me talk it over like old friends. Kate can't marry you, Mr. Severance. Is that plain? She can't marry you, and she can't marry anybody else. All I want is to spare her more scenes. Won't you take my word for it, and just slip off quietly if I promise you I'll make it all right, so she'll bear you no ill-will?'

I listened to this extraordinary proposal as composedly as I could; but it was impossible to repress a slight laugh. Miss Wilpert took my laugh for an answer, and her discoloured face crimsoned furiously. 'Well?'

'Nonsense, Miss Wilpert. Of course I won't take your orders to go away.'

She rested her elbows on the table, and her chin on her crossed hands. I saw she was making an immense effort to control herself. 'See here, young man, now you listen. . .'

Still I sat silent, and she sat looking at me, her thick lower lip groping queerly, as if it were feeling for words she could not find.

'I tell you –' she stammered.

I stood up. 'If vague threats are all you have to tell me, perhaps we'd better bring our talk to an end.'

She rose also. 'To an end? Any minute, if you'll agree to go away.'

'Can't you see that such arguments are wasted on me?'

'You mean to see her?'

'Of course I do – at once, if you'll excuse me.'

She drew back unsteadily, and put herself between me and the door. 'You're going to her now? But I tell you you can't! You'll half kill her. Is that what you're after?'

'What I'm after, first of all, is to put an end to this useless talk,' I said, moving toward the door. She flung herself heavily backward, and stood against it, stretching out her two arms to block my way. 'She can't marry – she can't marry you!' she screamed.

I stood silent, my hands in my pockets. 'You – you don't believe me?' she repeated.

'I've nothing more to say to you, Miss Wilpert.'

'Ah, you've nothing more to say to me? Is that the tune? Then I'll tell you that I've something more to say to you; and you're not going out of this room till you've heard it. And you'll wish you were dead when you have.'

'If it's anything about Mrs. Ingram, I refuse to hear it; and if you force me to, it will be exactly as if you were speaking to a man who's stone deaf. So you'd better ask yourself if it's worth while.'

She leaned against the door, her heavy head dropped queerly forward. 'Worth while – worth while? It'll be worth your while not to hear it – I'll give you a last chance,' she said.

'I should be much obliged if you'd leave my room, Miss Wilpert.'

'"Much obliged"?" she simpered, mimicking me. 'You'd be much obliged, would you? Hear him, girls – ain't he stylish? Well, I'm going to leave your room in a minute, young gentleman; but not till you've heard your death-sentence.'

I smiled. 'I shan't hear it, you know. I shall be stone deaf.'

She gave a little screaming laugh, and her arms dropped to her sides. 'Stone deaf, he says. And to the day of his death he'll never get out of his ears what I'm going to tell him. . .' She moved forward again, lurching a little; she seemed to be trying to take the few steps back to the table, and I noticed that she had left her hand-bag on it. I took it up. 'You want your bag?'

'My bag?' Her jaw fell slightly, and began to tremble again. 'Yes, yes . . . my bag . . . give it to me. Then you'll know all about Kate Spain. . .' She got as far as the armchair, dropped into it sideways, and sat with hanging head, and arms lolling at her sides. She seemed to have forgotten about the bag, though I had put it beside her.

I stared at her, horrified. Was she as drunk as all that – or was she ill, and desperately ill? I felt cold about the heart, and went up, and took hold of her. 'Miss Wilpert – won't you get up? Aren't you well?'

Her swollen lips formed a thin laugh, and I saw a thread of foam in their corners. 'Kate Spain. . . I'll tell you. . .' Her head sank down onto her creased white throat. Her arms hung lifeless; she neither spoke nor moved.

VIII

After the first moment of distress and bewilderment, and the two or three agitated hours spent in consultations, telephonings, engaging of nurses, and enquiring about nursing homes, I was at last able to have a few words with Mrs. Ingram.

Miss Wilpert's case was clear enough; a stroke produced by sudden excitement, which would certainly – as the doctors summoned from Milan advised us – result in softening of the brain, probably followed by death in a few weeks. The direct cause had been the poor woman's fit of rage against me; but the doctors told me privately that in her deteriorated condition any shock might have brought about the same result. Continual over-indulgence in food and drink – in drink especially – had made her, physiologically, an old woman before her time; all her organs were worn out, and the best that could be hoped was that the bodily resistance which sometimes develops when the mind fails would not keep her too long from dying.

I had to break this as gently as I could to Mrs. Ingram, and at the same time to defend myself against the painful inferences she might draw from the way in which the attack had happened. She knew – as the whole horrified *pension* knew – that Miss Wilpert had been taken suddenly ill in my room; and any one living on the same floor must have been aware that an angry discussion had preceded the attack. But Kate Ingram knew more; she, and she alone, knew why Cassie Wilpert had gone to my room, and when I found myself alone with her I instantly read that knowledge in her face. This being so, I thought it better to make no pretence.

'You saw Miss Wilpert, I suppose, before she came to me?' I asked.

She made a faint assenting motion; I saw that she was too shaken to speak.

'And she told you, probably, that she was going to tell me I must not marry you.'

'Yes – she told me.'

I sat down beside her and took her hand. 'I don't know what she meant,' I went on, 'or how she intended to prevent it; for before she could say anything more –'

Kate Ingram turned to me quickly. I could see the life rushing back to her stricken face. 'You mean – she didn't say anything more?'

'She had no time to.'

'Not a word more?'

'Nothing –'

Mrs. Ingram gave me one long look; then her head sank between her hands. I sat beside her in silence, and at last she dropped her hands and looked up again. 'You've been very good to me,' she said.

'Then, my dear, you must be good too. I want you to go to your room at once and take a long rest. Everything is arranged; the nurse has come. Early tomorrow morning the ambulance will be here. You can trust me to see that things are looked after.'

Her eyes rested on me, as if she were trying to grope for the thoughts beyond this screen of words. 'You're sure she said nothing more?' she repeated.

'On my honour, nothing.'

She got up and went obediently to her room.

It was perfectly clear to me that Mrs. Ingram's docility during those first grim days was due chiefly to the fact of her own helplessness. Little of the practical experience of every-day life had come into her melancholy existence, and I was not surprised that, in a strange country and among unfamiliar faces, she should turn to me for support. The shock of what had occurred, and God knows what secret dread behind it, had prostrated the poor creature, and the painful details still to be dealt with made my nearness a necessity. But, as far as our personal relations were concerned, I knew that sooner or later an emotional reaction would come.

For the moment it was kept off by other cares. Mrs. Ingram turned to me as to an old friend, and I was careful to make no other claim on her. She was installed at the nursing-home in Milan to which her companion had been transported; and I saw her there two or three times daily. Happily for the sick woman, the end was near; she never regained consciousness, and before the month was out she was dead. Her life ended without a struggle, and Mrs. Ingram was spared the sight of protracted suffering; but the shock of the separation was inevitable. I knew she did not love Cassie Wilpert, and I measured her profound isolation when I saw that the death of this woman left her virtually alone.

When we returned from the funeral I drove her back to the hotel where she had engaged rooms, and she asked me to come to see her there the next afternoon.

At Orta, after Cassie Wilpert's sudden seizure, and before the arrival of the doctors, I had handed her bag over to Mrs. Ingram, and had said: 'You'd better lock it up. If she gets worse the police might ask for it.'

She turned ashy pale. 'The police –?'

'Oh, you know there are endless formalities of that kind in all Latin countries. I should advise you to look through the bag yourself, and see if there's anything in it she might prefer not to have you keep. If there is, you'd better destroy it.'

I knew at the time that she had guessed I was referring to some particular paper; but she took the bag from me without speaking. And now, when I came to the hotel at her summons, I wondered whether she would allude to the matter, whether in the interval it had passed out of her mind, or whether she had decided to say nothing. There was no doubt that the bag had contained something which Miss Wilpert was determined that I should see; but, after all, it might have been only a newspaper report of the Spain trial. The unhappy creature's brain was already so confused that she might have attached importance to some document that had no real significance. I hoped it was so, for my one desire was to put out of my mind the memory of Cassie Wilpert, and of what her association with Mrs. Ingram had meant.

At the hotel I was asked to come up to Mrs. Ingram's private sitting-room. She kept me waiting for a little while, and when she appeared she looked so frail and ill in her black dress that I feared she might be on the verge of a nervous break-down.

'You look too tired to see any one today. You ought to go straight to bed and let me send for the doctor,' I said.

'No – no.' She shook her head, and signed to me to sit down. 'It's only ... the strangeness of everything. I'm not used to being alone. I think I'd better go away from here tomorrow,' she began excitedly.

'I think you had, dear. I'll make any arrangements you like, if you'll tell me where you want to go. And I'll come and join you, and arrange as soon as possible about our marriage. Such matters can be managed fairly quickly in France.'

'In France?' she echoed absently, with a little smile.

'Or wherever else you like. We might go to Rome.'

She continued to smile; a strained mournful smile, which began to frighten me. Then she spoke. 'I shall never forget what you've been to me. But we must say goodbye now. I can't marry you. Cassie did what was right – she only wanted to spare me the pain of telling you.'

I looked at her steadily. 'When you say you can't marry me,' I asked, 'do you mean that you're already married, and can't free yourself?'

She seemed surprised. 'Oh, no. I'm not married – I was never married.'

'Then, my dear –'

She raised one hand to silence me; with the other she opened her little black hand-bag and drew out a sealed envelope. 'This is the reason. It's what she meant to show you –'

I broke in at once: 'I don't want to see anything she meant to show me. I told her so then, and I tell you so now. Whatever is in that envelope, I refuse to look at it.'

Mrs. Ingram gave me a startled glance. 'No, no. You must read it. Don't force me to tell you – that would be worse. . .'

I jumped up and stood looking down into her anguished face. Even if I hadn't loved her, I should have pitied her then beyond all mortal pity.

'Kate,' I said, bending over her, and putting my hand on her icy-cold one, 'when I asked you to marry me I buried all such questions, and I'm not going to dig them up again today – or any other day. The past's the past. It's at an end for us both, and tomorrow I mean to marry you, and begin our future.'

She smiled again, strangely, I thought, and then suddenly began to cry. Then she flung her arms about my neck, and pressed herself against me. 'Say goodbye to me now – say goodbye to Kate Spain,' she whispered.

'Goodbye to Kate Spain, yes; but not to Kate Severance.'

'There'll never be a Kate Severance. There never can be. Oh, won't you understand – won't you spare me? Cassie was right; she tried to do her duty when she saw I couldn't do it. . .'

She broke into terrible sobs, and I pressed my lips against hers to silence her. She let me hold her for a while, and when she drew back from me I saw that the battle was half won. But she stretched out her hand toward the envelope. 'You must read it –'

I shook my head. 'I won't read it. But I'll take it and keep it. Will that satisfy you, Kate Severance?' I asked. For it had suddenly occurred to me that, if I tore the paper up before her, I should only force her, in her present mood, to the more cruel alternative of telling me what it contained.

I saw at once that my suggestion quieted her. 'You will take it, then? You'll read it tonight? You'll promise me?'

'No, my dear. All I promise you is to take it with me, and not to destroy it.'

She took a long sobbing breath, and drew me to her again. 'It's as if you'd read it already, isn't it?' she said below her breath.

'It's as if it had never existed – because it never will exist for me.' I held her fast, and kissed her again. And when I left her I carried the sealed envelope away with me.

IX

All that happened seven years ago; and the envelope lies before me now, still sealed. Why should I have opened it?

As I carried it home that night at Milan, as I drew it out of my pocket and locked it away among my papers, it was as transparent as glass to me. I had no need to open it. Already it had given me the measure of the woman who, deliberately, determinedly, had thrust it into my hands. Even as she was in the act of doing so, I had understood that with Cassie Wilpert's death the one danger she had to fear had been removed; and that, knowing herself at last free, at last safe, she had voluntarily placed her fate in my keeping.

'Greater love hath no man – certainly no woman,' I thought. Cassie Wilpert, and Cassie Wilpert alone, held Kate Spain's secret – the secret which would doubtless have destroyed her in the eyes of the world, as it was meant to destroy her in mine. And that secret, when it had been safely buried with Cassie Wilpert, Kate Spain had deliberately dug up again, and put into my hands.

It took her some time to understand the use I meant to make of it. She did not dream, at first, that it had given me a complete insight into her character, and that that was all I wanted of it. Weeks of patient waiting, of quiet reasoning, of obstinate insistence, were required to persuade her that I was determined to judge her, not by her past, whatever it might have been, but by what she had unconsciously revealed of herself since I had known her and loved her.

'You can't marry me – you know why you can't marry me,' she had gone on endlessly repeating; till one day I had turned on her, and declared abruptly: 'Whatever happens, this is to be our last talk on the subject. I will never return to it again, or let you return to it. But I swear one thing to you now; if you know how your father died, and have kept silence to shield some one – to shield I don't care who –' I looked straight into her eyes as I said this – 'if this is your reason for thinking you ought not to marry me, then I tell you now that it weighs nothing with me, and never will.'

She gave me back my look, long and deeply; then she bent and kissed my hands. That was all.

I had hazarded a great deal in saying what I did; and I knew the risk I was taking. It was easy to answer for the present; but how could I tell what the future, our strange incalculable future together, might bring? It was that which she dreaded, I knew; not for herself, but for me. But I was ready to risk it, and a few weeks after that final talk – for final I insisted on its being – I gained my point, and we were married.

We were married; and for five years we lived our strange perilous dream of happiness. That fresh unfading happiness which now and then mocks the lot of poor mortals; but not often – and never for long.

At the end of five years my wife died; and since then I have lived alone among memories so made of light and darkness that sometimes I am blind with remembered joy, and sometimes numb under present sorrow. I don't know yet which will end by winning the day with me; but in my uncertainty I am putting old things in order – and there on my desk lies the paper I have never read, and beside it the candle with which I shall presently burn it.

ROMAN FEVER

I

From the table at which they had been lunching two American ladies of ripe but well-cared-for middle age moved across the lofty terrace of the Roman restaurant and, leaning on its parapet, looked first at each other, and then down on the outspread glories of the Palatine and the Forum, with the same expression of vague but benevolent approval.

As they leaned there a girlish voice echoed up gaily from the stairs leading to the court below. 'Well, come along, then,' it cried, not to them but to an invisible companion, 'and let's leave the young things to their knitting'; and a voice as fresh laughed back: 'Oh, look here, Babs, not actually *knitting* –' 'Well, I mean figuratively,' rejoined the first. 'After all, we haven't left our poor parents much else to do. . .' and at that point the turn of the stairs engulfed the dialogue.

The two ladies looked at each other again, this time with a tinge of smiling embarrassment, and the smaller and paler one shook her head and coloured slightly.

'Barbara!' she murmured, sending an unheard rebuke after the mocking voice in the stairway.

The other lady, who was fuller, and higher in colour, with a small determined nose supported by vigorous black eyebrows, gave a good-humoured laugh. 'That's what our daughters think of us!'

Her companion replied by a deprecating gesture. 'Not of us individually. We must remember that. It's just the collective modern idea of Mothers. And you see –' Half guiltily she drew from her handsomely mounted black hand-bag a twist of crimson silk run through by two fine knitting needles. 'One never knows,' she murmured. 'The new system has certainly given us a good deal of time to kill; and sometimes I get tired just looking – even at this.' Her gesture was now addressed to the stupendous scene at their feet.

The dark lady laughed again, and they both relapsed upon the view, contemplating it in silence, with a sort of diffused serenity which might have been borrowed from the spring effulgence of the Roman skies. The luncheon-hour was long past, and the two had their end of the vast terrace to themselves. At its opposite extremity a few groups, detained by a lingering look at the outspread city, were gathering up guide-books and fumbling for tips. The last of them scattered, and the two ladies were alone on the air-washed height.

'Well, I don't see why we shouldn't just stay here,' said Mrs. Slade, the lady of the high colour and energetic brows. Two derelict basket-chairs stood near, and she pushed them into the angle of the parapet, and settled herself in one, her gaze upon the Palatine. 'After all, it's still the most beautiful view in the world.'

'It always will be, to me,' assented her friend Mrs. Ansley, with so slight a stress on the 'me' that Mrs. Slade, though she noticed it, wondered if it were not merely accidental, like the random underlinings of old-fashioned letter-writers.

'Grace Ansley was always old-fashioned,' she thought; and added aloud, with a retrospective smile: 'It's a view we've both been familiar with for a good many years. When we first met here we were younger than our girls are now. You remember?'

'Oh, yes, I remember,' murmured Mrs. Ansley, with the same undefinable stress. – 'There's that head-waiter wondering,' she interpolated. She was evidently far less sure than her companion of herself and of her rights in the world.

'I'll cure him of wondering,' said Mrs. Slade, stretching her hand toward a bag as discreetly opulent-looking as Mrs. Ansley's. Signing to the head-waiter, she explained that she and her friend were old lovers of Rome, and would like to spend the end of the afternoon looking down on the view – that is, if it did not disturb the service? The head-waiter, bowing over her gratuity, assured her that the ladies were most welcome, and would be still more so if they would condescend to remain for dinner. A full moon night, they would remember...

Mrs. Slade's black brows drew together, as though references to the moon were out-of-place and even unwelcome. But she smiled away her frown as the head-waiter retreated. 'Well, why not? We might do worse. There's no knowing, I suppose, when the girls will be back. Do you even know back from *where?* I don't!'

Mrs. Ansley again coloured slightly. 'I think those young Italian aviators we met at the Embassy invited them to fly to Tarquinia for tea. I suppose they'll want to wait and fly back by moonlight.'

'Moonlight – moonlight! What a part it still plays. Do you suppose they're as sentimental as we were?'

'I've come to the conclusion that I don't in the least know what they are,' said Mrs. Ansley. 'And perhaps we didn't know much more about each other.'

'No; perhaps we didn't.'

Her friend gave her a shy glance. 'I never should have supposed you were sentimental, Alida.'

'Well, perhaps I wasn't.' Mrs. Slade drew her lids together in retrospect; and for a few moments the two ladies, who had been intimate since childhood, reflected how little they knew each other. Each one, of course, had a label ready to attach to the other's name; Mrs. Delphin Slade, for instance, would have told herself, or any one who asked her, that Mrs. Horace Ansley, twenty-five years ago, had been exquisitely lovely – no, you wouldn't believe it, would you? . . . though, of course, still charming, distinguished. . . Well, as a girl she had been exquisite; far more beautiful than her daughter Barbara, though certainly Babs, according to the new standards at any rate, was more effective – had more *edge*, as they say. Funny where she got it, with those two nullities as parents. Yes; Horace Ansley was – well, just the duplicate of his wife. Museum specimens of old New York. Good-looking, irreproachable, exemplary. Mrs. Slade and Mrs. Ansley had lived opposite each other – actually as well as figuratively – for years. When the drawing-room curtains in No. 20 East 73rd Street were renewed, No. 23, across the way, was always aware of it. And of all the movings, buyings, travels, anniversaries, illnesses – the tame chronicle of an estimable pair. Little of it escaped Mrs. Slade. But she had grown bored with it by the time her husband made his big *coup* in Wall Street, and when they bought in upper Park Avenue had already begun to think: 'I'd rather live opposite a speak-easy for a change; at least one might see it raided.' The idea of seeing Grace raided was so amusing that (before the move) she launched it at a woman's lunch. It made a hit, and went the rounds – she sometimes wondered if it had crossed the street, and reached Mrs. Ansley. She hoped not, but didn't much mind. Those were the days when respectability was at a discount, and it did the irreproachable no harm to laugh at them a little.

A few years later, and not many months apart, both ladies lost their husbands. There was an appropriate exchange of wreaths and condolences, and a brief renewal of intimacy in the half-shadow of their mourning; and now, after another interval, they had run across each other in Rome, at the same hotel, each of them the modest appendage of a salient daughter. The similarity of their lot had again drawn them together, lending itself to mild jokes, and the mutual confession that, if in old days it must have been tiring to 'keep up' with daughters, it was now, at times, a little dull not to.

No doubt, Mrs. Slade reflected, she felt her unemployment more than poor Grace ever would. It was a big drop from being the wife of Delphin Slade to being his widow. She had always regarded herself (with a certain conjugal pride) as his equal in social gifts, as contributing her full share to the making of the exceptional couple they were: but the difference after his death was irremediable. As the wife of the famous corporation lawyer, always with an international case or two on hand, every day brought its exciting and unexpected obligation: the impromptu entertaining of eminent colleagues from abroad, the hurried dashes on legal business to London, Paris or Rome, where the entertaining was so handsomely reciprocated; the amusement of hearing in her wake: 'What, that handsome woman with the good clothes and the eyes is Mrs. Slade – *the* Slade's wife? Really? Generally the wives of celebrities are such frumps.'

Yes; being *the* Slade's widow was a dullish business after that. In living up to such a husband all her faculties had been engaged; now she had only her daughter to live up to, for the son who seemed to have inherited his father's gifts had died suddenly in boyhood. She had fought through that agony because her husband was there, to be helped and to help; now, after the father's death, the thought of the boy had become unbearable. There was nothing left but to mother her daughter; and dear Jenny was such a perfect daughter that she needed no excessive mothering. 'Now with Babs Ansley I don't know that I *should* be so quiet,' Mrs. Slade sometimes half-enviously reflected; but Jenny, who was younger than her brilliant friend, was that rare accident, an extremely pretty girl who somehow made youth and prettiness seem as safe as their absence. It was all perplexing – and to Mrs. Slade a little boring. She wished that Jenny would fall in love – with the wrong man, even; that she might have to be watched, out-manoeuvred, rescued. And instead, it was Jenny who watched her mother, kept her out of draughts, made sure that she had taken her tonic...

Mrs. Ansley was much less articulate than her friend, and her mental portrait of Mrs. Slade was slighter, and drawn with fainter touches. 'Alida Slade's awfully brilliant; but not as brilliant as she thinks,' would have summed it up; though she would have added, for the enlightenment of strangers, that Mrs. Slade had been an extremely dashing girl; much more so than her daughter, who was pretty, of course, and clever in a way, but had none of her mother's – well, 'vividness', some one had once called it. Mrs. Ansley would take up current words like this, and cite them in quotation marks, as unheard-of audacities. No; Jenny was not like her mother. Sometimes Mrs. Ansley thought Alida Slade was disappointed; on the whole she had had a sad life. Full of failures and mistakes; Mrs. Ansley had always been rather sorry for her. . .

So these two ladies visualised each other, each through the wrong end of her little telescope.

II

For a long time they continued to sit side by side without speaking. It seemed as though, to both, there was a relief in laying down their somewhat futile activities in the presence of the vast Memento Mori which faced them. Mrs. Slade sat quite still, her eyes fixed on the golden slope of the Palace of the Cæsars, and after a while Mrs. Ansley ceased to fidget with her bag, and she too sank into meditation. Like many intimate friends, the two ladies had never before had occasion to be silent together, and Mrs. Ansley was slightly embarrassed by what seemed, after so many years, a new stage in their intimacy, and one with which she did not yet know how to deal.

Suddenly the air was full of that deep clangour of bells which periodically covers Rome with a roof of silver. Mrs. Slade glanced at her wrist-watch. 'Five o'clock already,' she said, as though surprised.

Mrs. Ansley suggested interrogatively: 'There's bridge at the Embassy at five.' For a long time Mrs. Slade did not answer. She appeared to be lost in contemplation, and Mrs. Ansley thought the remark had escaped her. But after a while she said, as if speaking out of a dream: 'Bridge, did you say? Not unless you want to. . . But I don't think I will, you know.'

'Oh, no,' Mrs. Ansley hastened to assure her. 'I don't care to at all. It's so lovely here; and so full of old memories, as you say.' She settled herself in her chair, and almost furtively drew forth her knitting. Mrs. Slade took sideway note of this activity, but her own beautifully cared-for hands remained motionless on her knee.

'I was just thinking,' she said slowly, 'what different things Rome stands for to each generation of travellers. To our grandmothers, Roman fever; to our mothers, sentimental dangers – how we used to be guarded! – to our daughters, no more dangers than the middle of Main Street. They don't know it – ut how much they're missing!'

The long golden light was beginning to pale, and Mrs. Ansley lifted her knitting a little closer to her eyes. 'Yes; how we were guarded!'

'I always used to think,' Mrs. Slade continued, 'that our mothers had a much more difficult job than our grandmothers. When Roman fever stalked the streets it must have been comparatively easy to gather in the girls at the danger hour; but when you and I were young, with such beauty calling us, and the spice of disobedience thrown in, and no worse risk than catching cold during the cool hour after sunset, the mothers used to be put to it to keep us in – didn't they?'

She turned again toward Mrs. Ansley, but the latter had reached a delicate point in her knitting. 'One, two, three – slip two; yes, they must have been,' she assented, without looking up.

Mrs. Slade's eyes rested on her with a deepened attention. 'She can knit – in the face of *this*! How like her. . .'

Mrs. Slade leaned back, brooding, her eyes ranging from the ruins which faced her to the long green hollow of the Forum, the fading glow of the church fronts beyond it, and the outlying immensity of the Colosseum. Suddenly she thought: 'It's all very well to say that our girls have done away with sentiment and moonlight. But if Babs Ansley isn't out to catch that young aviator – the one who's a Marchese – then I don't know anything. And Jenny has no chance beside her. I know that too. I wonder if that's why Grace Ansley likes the two girls to go everywhere together? My poor Jenny as a foil –!' Mrs Slade gave a hardly audible laugh, and at the sound Mrs. Ansley dropped her knitting.

'Yes –?'

'I – oh, nothing. I was only thinking how your Babs carries everything before her. That Campolieri boy is one of the best matches in Rome. Don't look so innocent, my dear – you know he is. And I was wondering, ever so respectfully, you understand . . . wondering how two such exemplary characters as you and Horace had managed to produce anything quite so dynamic.' Mrs. Slade laughed again, with a touch of asperity.

Mrs. Ansley's hands lay inert across her needles. She looked straight out at the great accumulated wreckage of passion and splendour at her feet. But her small profile was almost expressionless. At length she said: 'I think you overrate Babs, my dear.'

Mrs. Slade's tone grew easier. 'No; I don't. I appreciate her. And perhaps envy you. Oh, my girl's perfect; if I were a chronic invalid I'd – well, I think I'd rather be in Jenny's hands. There must be times . . . but there! I always wanted a brilliant daughter . . . and never quite understood why I got an angel instead.'

Mrs. Ansley echoed her laugh in a faint murmur. 'Babs is an angel too.'

'Of course – of course! But she's got rainbow wings. Well, they're wandering by the sea with their young men; and here we sit . . . and it all brings back the past a little too acutely.'

Mrs. Ansley had resumed her knitting. One might almost have imagined (if one had known her less well, Mrs. Slade reflected) that, for her also, too many memories rose from the lengthening shadows of those august ruins. But no; she was simply absorbed in her work. What was there for her to worry about? She knew that Babs would almost certainly come back engaged to the extremely eligible Campolieri. 'And she'll sell the New York house, and settle down near them in Rome, and never be in their way . . . she's much too tactful. But she'll have an excellent cook, and just the right people in for bridge and cocktails . . . and a perfectly peaceful old age among her grandchildren.'

Mrs. Slade broke off this prophetic flight with a recoil of self-disgust. There was no one of whom she had less right to think unkindly than of Grace Ansley. Would she never cure herself of envying her? Perhaps she had begun too long ago.

She stood up and leaned against the parapet, filling her troubled eyes with the tranquillizing magic of the hour. But instead of tranquillizing her the sight seemed to increase her exasperation. Her gaze turned toward the Colosseum. Already its golden flank was drowned in purple shadow, and above it the sky curved crystal clear, without light or colour. It was the moment when afternoon and evening hang balanced in mid-heaven.

Mrs. Slade turned back and laid her hand on her friend's arm. The gesture was so abrupt that Mrs. Ansley looked up, startled.

'The sun's set. You're not afraid, my dear?'

'Afraid –?'

'Of Roman fever or pneumonia? I remember how ill you were that winter. As a girl you had a very delicate throat, hadn't you?'

'Oh, we're all right up here. Down below, in the Forum, it does get deathly cold, all of a sudden . . . but not here.'

'Ah, of course you know because you had to be so careful.' Mrs Slade turned back to the parapet. She thought: 'I must make one more effort not to hate her.' Aloud she said: 'Whenever I look at the Forum from up here, I remember that story about a great-aunt of yours, wasn't she? A dreadfully wicked great-aunt?'

'Oh, yes; Great-aunt Harriet. The one who was supposed to have sent her young sister out to the Forum after sunset to gather a night-blooming flower for her album. All our great-aunts and grandmothers used to have albums of dried flowers.'

Mrs. Slade nodded. 'But she really sent her because they were in love with the same man –'

'Well, that was the family tradition. They said Aunt Harriet confessed it years afterward. At any rate, the poor little sister caught the fever and died. Mother used to frighten us with the story when we were children.'

'And you frightened *me* with it, that winter when you and I were here as girls. The winter I was engaged to Delphin.'

Mrs. Ansley gave a faint laugh. 'Oh, did I? Really frightened you? I don't believe you're easily frightened.'

'Not often; but I was then. I was easily frightened because I was too happy. I wonder if you know what that means?'

'I – yes . . .' Mrs. Ansley faltered.

'Well, I suppose that was why the story of your wicked aunt made such an impression on me. And I thought: 'There's no more Roman fever, but the Forum is deathly cold after sunset – especially after a hot day. And the Colosseum's even colder and damper.'

'The Colosseum –?'

'Yes. It wasn't easy to get in, after the gates were locked for the night. Far from easy. Still, in those days it could be managed; it *was* managed, often. Lovers met there who couldn't meet elsewhere. You knew that?'

'I – I daresay. I don't remember.'

'You don't remember? You don't remember going to visit some ruins or other one evening, just after dark, and catching a bad chill? You were supposed to have gone to see the moon rise. People always said that expedition was what caused your illness.'

There was a moment's silence; then Mrs. Ansley rejoined: 'Did they? It was all so long ago.'

'Yes. And you got well again – so it didn't matter. But I suppose it struck your friends – the reason given for your illness, I mean – because everybody knew you were so prudent on account of your throat, and your mother took such care of you. . . You *had* been out late sight-seeing, hadn't you, that night?'

'Perhaps I had. The most prudent girls aren't always prudent. What made you think of it now?'

Mrs. Slade seemed to have no answer ready. But after a moment she broke out: 'Because I simply can't bear it any longer –!'

Mrs. Ansley lifted her head quickly. Her eyes were wide and very pale. 'Can't bear what?'

'Why – your not knowing that I've always known why you went.'

'Why I went –?'

'Yes. You think I'm bluffing, don't you? Well, you went to meet the man I was engaged to – and I can repeat every word of the letter that took you there.'

While Mrs. Slade spoke Mrs. Ansley had risen unsteadily to her feet. Her bag, her knitting and gloves, slid in a panic-stricken heap to the ground. She looked at Mrs. Slade as though she were looking at a ghost.

'No, no – don't,' she faltered out.

'Why not? Listen, if you don't believe me. 'My one darling, things can't go on like this. I must see you alone. Come to the Colosseum immediately after dark tomorrow. There will be somebody to let you in. No one whom you need fear will suspect' – but perhaps you've forgotten what the letter said?'

Mrs. Ansley met the challenge with an unexpected composure. Steadying herself against the chair she looked at her friend, and replied: 'No; I know it by heart too.'

'And the signature? 'Only *your* D.S.' Was that it? I'm right, am I? That was the letter that took you out that evening after dark?'

Mrs. Ansley was still looking at her. It seemed to Mrs. Slade that a slow struggle was going on behind the voluntarily controlled mask of her small quiet face. 'I shouldn't have thought she had herself so well in hand,' Mrs. Slade reflected, almost resentfully. But at this moment Mrs. Ansley spoke. 'I don't know how you knew. I burnt that letter at once.'

'Yes; you would, naturally – you're so prudent!' The sneer was open now. 'And if you burnt the letter you're wondering how on earth I know what was in it. That's it, isn't it?'

Mrs. Slade waited, but Mrs. Ansley did not speak.

'Well, my dear, I know what was in that letter because I wrote it!'

'You wrote it?'

'Yes.'

The two women stood for a minute staring at each other in the last golden light. Then Mrs. Ansley dropped back into her chair. 'Oh,' she murmured, and covered her face with her hands.

Mrs. Slade waited nervously for another word or movement. None came, and at length she broke out: 'I horrify you.'

Mrs. Ansley's hands dropped to her knee. The face they uncovered was streaked with tears. 'I wasn't thinking of you. I was thinking – it was the only letter I ever had from him!'

'And I wrote it. Yes; I wrote it! But I was the girl he was engaged to. Did you happen to remember that?'

Mrs. Ansley's head drooped again. 'I'm not trying to excuse myself. . . I remembered. . .'

'And still you went?'

'Still I went.'

Mrs. Slade stood looking down on the small bowed figure at her side. The flame of her wrath had already sunk, and she wondered why she had ever thought there would be any satisfaction in inflicting so purposeless a wound on her friend. But she had to justify herself.

'You do understand? I'd found out – and I hated you, hated you. I knew you were in love with Delphin – and I was afraid; afraid of you, of your quiet ways, your sweetness . . . your . . . well, I wanted you out of the way, that's all. Just for a few weeks; just till I was sure of him. So in a blind fury I wrote that letter. . . I don't know why I'm telling you now.'

'I suppose,' said Mrs. Ansley slowly, 'it's because you've always gone on hating me.'

'Perhaps. Or because I wanted to get the whole thing off my mind.' She paused. 'I'm glad you destroyed the letter. Of course I never thought you'd die.'

Mrs. Ansley relapsed into silence, and Mrs. Slade, leaning above her, was conscious of a strange sense of isolation, of being cut off from the warm current of human communion. 'You think me a monster!'

'I don't know. . . It was the only letter I had, and you say he didn't write it?'

'Ah, how you care for him still!'

'I cared for that memory,' said Mrs. Ansley.

Mrs. Slade continued to look down on her. She seemed physically reduced by the blow – as if, when she got up, the wind might scatter her like a puff of dust. Mrs. Slade's jealousy suddenly leapt up again at the sight. All these years the woman had been living on that letter. How she must have loved him, to treasure the mere memory of its ashes! The letter of the man her friend was engaged to. Wasn't it she who was the monster?

'You tried your best to get him away from me, didn't you? But you failed; and I kept him. That's all.'

'Yes. That's all.'

'I wish now I hadn't told you. I'd no idea you'd feel about it as you do; I thought you'd be amused. It all happened so long ago, as you say; and you must do me the justice to remember that I had no reason to think you'd ever taken it seriously. How could I, when you were married to Horace Ansley two months afterward? As soon as you could get out of bed your mother rushed you off to Florence and married you. People were rather surprised – they wondered at its being done so quickly; but I thought I knew. I had an idea you did it out of *pique* – to be able to say you'd got ahead of Delphin and me. Girls have such silly reasons for doing the most serious things. And your marrying so soon convinced me that you'd never really cared.'

'Yes. I suppose it would,' Mrs. Ansley assented.

The clear heaven overhead was emptied of all its gold. Dusk spread over it, abruptly darkening the Seven Hills. Here and there lights began to twinkle through the foliage at their feet. Steps were coming and going on the deserted terrace – waiters looking out of the doorway at the head of the stairs, then reappearing with trays and napkins and flasks of wine. Tables were moved, chairs straightened. A feeble string of electric lights flickered out. Some vases of faded flowers were carried away, and brought back replenished. A stout lady in a dust-coat suddenly appeared, asking in broken Italian if any one had seen the elastic band which held together her tattered Baedeker. She poked with her stick under the table at which she had lunched, the waiters assisting.

The corner where Mrs. Slade and Mrs. Ansley sat was still shadowy and deserted. For a long time neither of them spoke. At length Mrs. Slade began again: 'I suppose I did it as a sort of joke –'

'A joke?'

'Well, girls are ferocious sometimes, you know. Girls in love especially. And I remember laughing to myself all that evening at the idea that you were waiting around there in the dark, dodging out of sight, listening for every sound, trying to get in –. Of course I was upset when I heard you were so ill afterward.'

Mrs. Ansley had not moved for a long time. But now she turned slowly toward her companion. 'But I didn't wait. He'd arranged everything. He was there. We were let in at once,' she said.

Mrs. Slade sprang up from her leaning position. 'Delphin there? They let you in? – Ah, now you're lying!' she burst out with violence.

Mrs. Ansley's voice grew clearer, and full of surprise. 'But of course he was there. Naturally he came –'

'Came? How did he know he'd find you there? You must be raving!'

Mrs. Ansley hesitated, as though reflecting. 'But I answered the letter. I told him I'd be there. So he came.'

Mrs. Slade flung her hands up to her face. 'Oh, God – you answered! I never thought of your answering. . .'

'It's odd you never thought of it, if you wrote the letter.'

'Yes. I was blind with rage.'

Mrs. Ansley rose, and drew her fur scarf about her. 'It is cold here. We'd better go. . . I'm sorry for you,' she said, as she clasped the fur about her throat.

The unexpected words sent a pang through Mrs. Slade. 'Yes; we'd better go.' She gathered up her bag and cloak. 'I don't know why you should be sorry for me,' she muttered.

Mrs. Ansley stood looking away from her toward the dusky secret mass of the Colosseum. 'Well – because I didn't have to wait that night.'

Mrs. Slade gave an unquiet laugh. 'Yes; I was beaten there. But I oughtn't to begrudge it to you, I suppose. At the end of all these years. After all, I had everything; I had him for twenty-five years. And you had nothing but that one letter that he didn't write.'

Mrs. Ansley was again silent. At length she turned toward the door of the terrace. She took a step, and turned back, facing her companion.

'I had Barbara,' she said, and began to move ahead of Mrs. Slade toward the stairway.

THE LOOKING-GLASS

I

Mrs. Attlee had never been able to understand why there was any harm in giving people a little encouragement when they needed it.

Sitting back in her comfortable armchair by the fire, her working-days over, and her muscular masseuse's hands lying swollen and powerless on her knee, she was at leisure to turn the problem over, and ponder it as there had never been time to do before.

Mrs. Attlee was so infirm now that, when her widowed daughter-in-law was away for the day, her granddaughter Moyra Attlee had to stay with her until the kitchen-girl had prepared the cold supper, and could come in and sit in the parlour.

'You'd be surprised, you know, my dear, to find how discouraged the grand people get, in those big houses with all the help, and the silver dinner plates, and a bell always handy if the fire wants poking, or the pet dog asks for a drink. . . And what'd a masseuse be good for, if she didn't jolly up their minds a little along with their muscles? – as Dr. Welbridge used to say to me many a time, when he'd given me a difficult patient. And he always gave me the most difficult,' she added proudly.

She paused, aware (for even now little escaped her) that Moyra had ceased to listen, but accepting the fact resignedly, as she did most things in the slow decline of her days.

'It's a fine afternoon,' she reflected, 'and likely she's fidgety because there's a new movie on; or that young fellow's fixed it up to get back earlier from New York. . .'

She relapsed into silence, following her thoughts; but presently, as happens with old people, they came to the surface again.

'And I hope I'm a good Catholic, as I said to Father Divott the other day, and at peace with heaven, if ever I was took suddenly – but no matter what happens I've got to risk my punishment for the wrong I did to Mrs. Clingsland, because as long as I've never repented it there's no use telling Father Divott about it. Is there?'

Mrs. Attlee heaved an introspective sigh. Like many humble persons of her kind and creed, she had a vague idea that a sin unrevealed was, as far as the consequences went, a sin uncommitted; and this conviction had often helped her in the difficult task of reconciling doctrine and practice.

II

Moyra Attlee interrupted her listless stare down the empty Sunday street of the New Jersey suburb, and turned an astonished glance on her grandmother.

'Mrs. Clingsland? A wrong you did to Mrs. Clingsland?'

Hitherto she had lent an inattentive ear to her grandmother's ramblings; the talk of old people seemed to be a language hardly worth learning. But it was not always so with Mrs. Attlee's. Her activities among the rich had ceased before the first symptoms of the financial depression; but her tenacious memory was stored with pictures of the luxurious days of which her granddaughter's generation, even in a wider world, knew only by hearsay. Mrs. Attlee had a gift for evoking in a few words scenes of half-understood opulence and leisure, like a guide leading a stranger through the gallery of a palace in the twilight, and now and then lifting a lamp to a shimmering Rembrandt or a jewelled Rubens; and it was particularly when she mentioned Mrs. Clingsland that Moyra caught these dazzling glimpses. Mrs. Clingsland had always been something more than a name to the Attlee family. They knew (though they did not know why) that it was through her help that Grandmother Attlee had been able, years ago, to buy the little house at Montclair, with a patch of garden behind it, where, all through the depression, she had held out, thanks to fortunate investments made on the advice of Mrs. Clingsland's great friend, the banker.

'She had so many friends, and they were all high-up people, you understand. Many's the time she'd say to me: 'Cora' (think of the loveliness of her calling me Cora), 'Cora, I'm going to buy some Golden Flyer shares on Mr. Stoner's advice; Mr. Stoner of the National Union Bank, you know. He's getting me in on the ground floor, as they say, and if you want to step in with me, why come along. There's nothing too good for you, in my opinion,' she used to say. And, as it turned out, those shares have kept their head above water all through the bad years, and now I think they'll see me through, and be there when I'm gone, to help out you children.'

Today Moyra Attlee heard the revered name with a new interest. The phrase: 'The wrong I did to Mrs. Clingsland,' had struck through her listlessness, rousing her to sudden curiosity. What could her grandmother mean by saying she had done a wrong to the benefactress whose bounties she was never tired of recording? Moyra believed her grandmother to be a very good woman – certainly she had been wonderfully generous in all her dealings with her children and grandchildren; and it seemed incredible that, if there had been one grave lapse in her life, it should have taken the form of an injury to Mrs. Clingsland. True, whatever the lapse was, she seemed to have made peace with herself about it; yet it was clear that its being unconfessed lurked disquietingly in the back of her mind.

'How can you say you ever did harm to a friend like Mrs. Clingsland, Gran?'

Mrs. Attlee's eyes grew sharp behind her spectacles, and she fixed them half distrustfully on the girl's face. But in a moment she seemed to recover herself. 'Not harm, I don't say; I'll never think I harmed her. Bless you, it wasn't to harm her I'd ever have lifted a finger. All I wanted was to help. But when you try to help too many people at once, the devil sometimes takes note of it. You see, there's quotas nowadays for everything, doing good included, my darling.'

Moyra made an impatient movement. She did not care to hear her grandmother philosophise. 'Well – but you said you did a wrong to Mrs. Clingsland.'

Mrs. Attlee's sharp eyes seemed to draw back behind a mist of age. She sat silent, her hands lying heavily over one another in their tragic uselessness.

'What would *you* have done, I wonder,' she began suddenly, 'if you'd ha' come in on her that morning, and seen her laying in her lovely great bed, with the lace a yard deep on the sheets, and her face buried in the pillows, so I knew she was crying? Would you have opened your bag same as usual, and got out your cocoanut cream and talcum powder, and the nail polishers, and all the rest of it, and waited there like a statute till she turned over to you; or'd you have gone up to her, and turned her softly round, like you would a baby, and said to her: 'Now, my dear, I guess you can tell Cora Attlee what's the trouble'? Well, that's what I did, anyhow; and there she was, with her face streaming with tears, and looking like a martyred saint on an altar, and when I said to her: 'Come, now, you tell me, and it'll help you,' she just sobbed out: 'Nothing can ever help me, now I've lost it.'

' 'Lost what?' I said, thinking first of her boy, the Lord help me, though I'd heard him whistling on the stairs as I went up; but she said: 'My beauty, Cora – I saw it suddenly slipping out of the door from me this morning'. . . Well, at that I had to laugh, and half angrily too. 'Your beauty,' I said to her, 'and is that all? And me that thought it was your husband, or your son – or your fortune even. If it's only your beauty, can't I give it back to you with these hands of mine? But what are you saying to me about beauty, with that seraph's face looking up at me this minute?' I said to her, for she angered me as if she'd been blaspheming.'

'Well, was it true?' Moyra broke in, impatient and yet curious.

'True that she'd lost her beauty?' Mrs. Attlee paused to consider. 'Do you know how it is, sometimes when you're doing a bit of fine darning, sitting by the window in the afternoon; and one minute it's full daylight, and your needle seems to find the way of itself; and the next minute you say: 'Is it my eyes?' because the work seems blurred; and presently you see it's the daylight going, stealing away, soft-like, from your corner, though there's plenty left overhead. Well – it was that way with her. . .'

But Moyra had never done fine darning, or strained her eyes in fading light, and she intervened again, more impatiently: 'Well, what did she do?'

Mrs. Attlee once more reflected. 'Why, she made me tell her every morning that it wasn't true; and every morning she believed me a little less. And she asked everybody in the house, beginning with her husband, poor man – him so bewildered when you asked him anything outside of his business, or his club or his horses, and never noticing any difference in her looks since the day he'd led her home as his bride, twenty years before, maybe. . .

'But there – nothing he could have said, if he'd had the wit to say it, would have made any difference. From the day she saw the first little line around her eyes she thought of herself as an old woman, and the thought never left her for more than a few minutes at a time. Oh, when she was dressed up, and laughing, and receiving company; then I don't say the faith in her beauty wouldn't come back to her, and go to her head like champagne; but it wore off quicker than champagne, and I've seen her run upstairs with the foot of a girl, and then, before she'd tossed off her finery, sit down in a heap in front of one of her big looking-glasses – it was looking-glasses everywhere in her room – and stare and stare till the tears ran down over her powder.'

'Oh, well, I suppose it's always hateful growing old,' said Moyra, her indifference returning.

Mrs. Attlee smiled retrospectively. 'How can I say that, when my own old age has been made so peaceful by all her goodness to me?'

Moyra stood up with a shrug. 'And yet you tell me you acted wrong to her. How am I to know what you mean?'

Her grandmother made no answer. She closed her eyes, and leaned her head against the little cushion behind her neck. Her lips seemed to murmur, but no words came. Moyra reflected that she was probably falling asleep, and that when she woke she would not remember what she had been about to reveal.

'It's not much fun sitting here all this time, if you can't even keep awake long enough to tell me what you mean about Mrs. Clingsland,' she grumbled.

Mrs. Attlee roused herself with a start.

III

Well (she began) you know what happened in the war – I mean, the way all the fine ladies, and the poor shabby ones too, took to running to the mediums and the *clair-voyants*, or whatever the stylish folk call 'em. The women had to have news of their men; and they were made to pay high enough for it. . . Oh, the stories I used to hear – and the price paid wasn't only money, either! There was a fair lot of swindlers and blackmailers in the business, there was. I'd sooner have trusted a gypsy at a fair. . . But the women just *had* to go to them.

Well, my dear, I'd always had a way of seeing things; from the cradle, even. I don't mean reading the tea-leaves, or dealing the cards; that's for the kitchen. No, no; I mean, feeling there's things about you, behind you, whispering over your shoulder. . . Once my mother, on the Connemara hills, saw the leprechauns at dusk; and she said they smelt fine and high, too. . . Well, when I used to go from one grand house to another, to give my massage and face-treatment, I got more and more sorry for those poor wretches that the sooth-saying swindlers were dragging the money out of for a pack of lies; and one day I couldn't stand it any longer, and though I knew the Church was against it, when I saw one lady nearly crazy, because for months she'd had no news of her boy at the front, I said to her: 'If you'll come over to my place tomorrow, I might have a word for you.' And the wonder of it was that I *had*! For that night I dreamt a message came saying there was good news for her, and the next day, sure enough, she had a cable, telling her her son had escaped from a German camp. . .

After that the ladies came in flocks – in flocks fairly. . . You're too young to remember, child; but your mother could tell you. Only she wouldn't, because after a bit the priest got wind of it, and then it had to stop . . . so she won't even talk of it any more. But I always said: How could I help it? For I *did* see things, and hear things, at that time. . . And of course the ladies were supposed to come just for the face-treatment . . . and was I to blame if I kept hearing those messages for them, poor souls, or seeing things they wanted me to see?

It's no matter now, for I made it all straight with Father Divott years ago; and now nobody comes after me any more, as you can see for yourself. And all I ask is to be left alone in my chair. . .

But with Mrs. Clingsland – well, that was different. To begin with, she was the patient I liked best. There was nothing she wouldn't do for you, if ever for a minute you could get her to stop thinking of herseif . . . and that's saying a good deal, for a rich lady. Money's an armour, you see; and there's few cracks in it.

But Mrs. Clingsland was a loving nature, if only anybody'd shown her how to love. . . Oh, dear, and wouldn't she have been surprised if you'd told her that! Her that thought she was living up to her chin in love and love-making. But as soon as the lines began to come about her eyes, she didn't believe in it any more. And she had to be always hunting for new people to tell her she was as beautiful as ever; because she wore the others out, forever asking them: 'Don't you think I'm beginning to go off a little?' – till finally fewer and fewer came to the house, and as far as a poor masseuse like me can judge, I didn't much fancy the looks of those that did; and I saw Mr. Clingsland didn't either.

But there was the children, you'll say. I know, I know! And she did love her children in a way; only it wasn't their way. The girl, who was a good bit the eldest, took after her father: a plain face and plain words. Dogs and horses and athletics. With her mother she was cold and scared; so her mother was cold and scared with her. The boy was delicate when he was little, so she could curl him up, and put him into black velvet pants, like that boy in the book – little Lord Something. But when his long legs grew out of the pants, and they sent him to school, she said he wasn't her own little coodly baby any more; and it riles a growing boy to hear himself talked about like that.

She had good friends left, of course; mostly elderly ladies they were, of her own age (for she *was* elderly now; the change had come), who used to drop in often for a gossip; but, bless your heart, they weren't much help, for what she wanted, and couldn't do without, was the gaze of men Struck dumb by her beauty. And that was what she couldn't get any longer, except she paid for it. And even so –!

For, you see, she was too quick and clever to be humbugged long by the kind that tried to get things out of her. How she used to laugh at the old double-chinners trotting round to the night-clubs with their boy friends! She laughed at old ladies in love;

and yet she couldn't bear to be out of love, though she knew she was getting to be an old lady herself.

Well, I remember one day another patient of mine, who'd never had much looks beyond what you can buy in Fifth Avenue, laughing at me about Mrs. Clingsland, about her dread of old age, and her craze for admiration – and as I listened, I suddenly thought: 'Why, we don't either of us know anything about what a beautiful woman suffers when she loses her beauty. For you and me, and thousands like us, beginning to grow old is like going from a bright warm room to one a little less warm and bright; but to a beauty like Mrs. Clingsland it's like being pushed out of an illuminated ball-room, all flowers and chandeliers, into the winter night and the snow.' And I had to bite the words back, not to say them to my patient. . .

IV

Mrs. Clingsland brightened up a little when her own son grew up and went to College. She used to go over and see him now and again; or he'd come home for the holidays. And he used to take her out for lunch, or to dance at those cabaret places; and when the head-waiters took her for his sweetheart she'd talk about it for a week. But one day a hall porter said: 'Better hurry up, mister. There's your mother waiting for you over there, looking clean fagged out'; and after that she didn't go round with him so much.

For a time she used to get some comfort out of telling me about her early triumphs; and I used to listen patiently, because I knew it was safer for her to talk to me than to the flatterers who were beginning to get round her.

You mustn't think of her, though, as an unkind woman. She was friendly to her husband, and friendly to her children; but they meant less and less to her. What she wanted was a looking-glass to stare into; and when her own people took enough notice of her to serve as looking-glasses, which wasn't often, she didn't much fancy what she saw there. I think this was about the worst time of her life. She lost a tooth; she began to dye her hair; she went into retirement to have her face lifted, and then got frightened, and came out again looking like a ghost, with a pouch under one eye, where they'd begun the treatment. . .

I began to be really worried about her then. She got sour and bitter toward everybody, and I seemed to be the only person she could talk out to. She used to keep me by her for hours, always paying for the appointments she made me miss, and going over the same thing again and again; how when she was young and came into a ball-room, or a restaurant or a theatre, everybody stopped what they were doing to turn and look at her – even the actors on the stage did, she said; and it was the truth, I daresay. But that was over. . .

Well, what could I say to her? She'd heard it all often enough. But there were people prowling about in the background that I didn't like the look of; people, you understand, who live on weak women that can't grow old. One day she showed me a love-letter. She said she didn't know the man who'd sent it; but she knew about him. He was a Count Somebody; a foreigner. He'd had adventures. Trouble in his own country, I guess. . . She laughed and tore the letter up. Another came from him, and I saw that too – but I didn't see her tear it up.

'Oh, I know what he's after,' she said. 'Those kind of men are always looking out for silly old women with money. . . Ah,' says she, 'it was different in old times. I remember one day I'd gone into a florist's to buy some violets, and I saw a young fellow there; well, maybe he was a little younger than me – but I looked like a girl still. And when he saw me he just stopped short with what he was saying to the florist, and his face turned so white I thought he was going to faint. I bought my violets; and as I went out a violet dropped from the bunch, and I saw him stoop and pick it up, and hide it away as if it had been money he'd stolen... Well,' she says, 'a few days after that I met him at a dinner, and it turned out he was the son of a friend of mine, a woman older than myself, who'd married abroad. He'd been brought up in England, and had just come to New York to take up a job there...'

She lay back with her eyes closed, and a quiet smile on her poor tormented face. 'I didn't know it then, but I suppose that was the only time I've ever been in love...' For a while she didn't say anything more, and I noticed the tears beginning to roll down her cheeks. 'Tell me about it, now do, you poor soul,' I says; for I thought, this is better for her than fandangoing with that oily Count whose letter she hasn't torn up.

'There's so little to tell,' she said. 'We met only four or five times – and then Harry went down on the *Titanic*.'

'Mercy,' says I, 'and was it all those years ago?'

'The years don't make any difference, Cora,' she says. 'The way he looked at me I know no one ever worshipped me as he did.'

'And did he tell you so?' I went on, humouring her; though I felt kind of guilty toward her husband.

'Some things don't have to be told,' says she, with the smile of a bride. 'If only he hadn't died, Cora... It's the sorrowing for him that's made me old before my time.' (Before her time! And her well over fifty.)

Well, a day or two after that I got a shock. Coming out of Mrs. Clingsland's front door as I was going into it I met a woman I'd know among a million if I was to meet her again in hell – where I will, I know, if I don't mind my Steps... You see, Moyra, though I broke years ago with all that crystal-reading, and table-rapping, and what the Church forbids, I was mixed up in it for a time (till Father Divott ordered me to stop), and I knew, by sight at any rate, most of the big mediums and their touts. And this woman on the doorstep was a tout, one of the worst and most notorious in New York; I knew cases where she'd sucked people dry selling them the news they wanted, like she was selling them a forbidden drug. And all of a sudden it came to me that I'd heard it said that she kept a foreign Count, who was sucking *her* dry – and I gave one jump home to my own place, and sat down there to think it over.

I saw well enough what was going to happen. Either she'd persuade my poor lady that the Count was mad over her beauty, and get a hold over her that way; or else – and this was worse – she'd make Mrs. Clingsland talk, and get at the story of the poor young man called Harry, who was drowned, and bring her messages from him; and that might go on forever, and bring in more money than the Count. . .

Well, Moyra, could *I* help it? I was so sorry for her, you see. I could see she was sick and fading away, and her will weaker than it used to be; and if I was to save her from those gangsters I had to do it right away, and make it straight with my conscience afterward – if I could. . .

V

I don't believe I ever did such hard thinking as I did that night. For what was I after doing? Something that was against my Church and against my own principles; and if ever I got found out, it was all up with me – me, with my thirty years' name of being the best masseuse in New York, and none honester, nor more respectable!

Well, then, I says to myself, what'll happen if that woman gets hold of Mrs. Clingsland? Why, one way or another, she'll bleed her white, and then leave her without help or comfort. I'd seen households where that had happened, and I wasn't going to let it happen to my poor lady. What I was after was to make her believe in herself again, so that she'd be in a kindlier mind toward others . . . and by the next day I'd thought my plan out, and set it going.

It wasn't so easy, neither; and I sometimes wonder at my nerve. I'd figured it out that the other woman would have to work the stunt of the young man who was drowned, because I was pretty sure Mrs. Clingsland, at the last minute, would shy away from the Count. Well, then, thinks I, I'll work the same stunt myself – but how?

You see, dearie, those big people, when they talk and write to each other, they use lovely words we ain't used to; and I was afraid if I began to bring messages to her, I'd word them wrong, and she'd suspect something. I knew I could work it the first day or the second; but after that I wasn't so sure. But there was no time to lose, and when I went back to her next morning I said: 'A queer thing happened to me last night. I guess it was the way you spoke to me about that gentleman – the one on the *Titanic*. Making me see him as clear as if he was in the room with us –' and at that I had her sitting up in bed with her great eyes burning into me like gimlets. 'Oh, Cora, perhaps he *is*! Oh, tell me quickly what happened!'

'Well, when I was laying in my bed last night something came to me from him. I knew at once it was from him; it was a word he was telling me to bring you. . .'

I had to wait then, she was crying so hard, before she could listen to me again; and when I went on she hung on to me, saving the word, as if I'd been her Saviour. The poor woman!

The message I'd hit on for that first day was easy enough. I said he'd told me to tell her he'd always loved her. It went down her throat like honey, and she just lay there and tasted it. But after a while she lifted up her head. 'Then why didn't he teil me so?' says she.

'Ah,' says I, 'I'll have to try to reach him again, and ask him that.' And that day she fairly drove me off on my other jobs, for fear I'd be late getting home, and too tired to hear him if he came again. 'And he *will* come, Cora; I know he will! And you must be ready for him, and write down everything. I want every word written down the minute he says it, for fear you'll forget a Single one.'

Well, that was a new difficulty. Writing wasn't ever my strong point; and when it came to finding the words for a young gentleman in love who'd gone down on the *Titanic*, you might as well have asked me to write a Chinese dictionary. Not that *I* couldn't imagine how he'd have felt; but I didn't for Mary's grace know how to say it for him.

But it's wonderful, as Father Divott says, how Providence sometimes seems to be listening behind the door. That night when I got home I found a message from a patient, asking me to go to see a poor young fellow she'd befriended when she was better off – he'd been her children's tutor, I believe – who was down and out, and dying in a miserable rooming-house down here at Montclair. Well, I went; and I saw at once why he hadn't kept this job, or any other job. Poor fellow, it was the drink; and now he was dying of it. It was a pretty bad Story, but there's only a bit of it belongs to what I'm telling you.

He was a highly educated gentleman, and as quick as a flash; and before I'd half explained, he told me what to say, and wrote out the message for me. I remember it now. 'He was so blinded by your beauty that he couldn't speak – and when he saw you the next time, at that dinner, in your bare shoulders and your pearls, he felt farther away from you than ever. And he walked the streets till morning, and then went home, and wrote you a letter; but he didn't dare to send it after all.'

This time Mrs. Clingsland swallowed it down like *champagne*. Blinded by her beauty; struck dumb by love of her! Oh, but that's what she'd been thirsting and hungering for all these years. Only, once it had begun, she had to have more of it, and always more . . . and my job didn't get any easier.

Luckily, though, I had that young fellow to help me; and after a while, when I'd given him a hint of what it was all about, he got as much interested as I was, and began to fret for me the days I didn't come.

But, my, what questions she *asked*. 'Tell him, if it's true that I took his breath away that first evening at dinner, to describe to you how I was dressed. They must remember things like that even in the other world, don't you think so? And you say he noticed my pearls?'

Luckily she'd described that dress to me so often that I had no difficulty about telling the young man what to say – and so it went on, and it went on, and one way or another I managed each time to have an answer that satisfied her. But one day, after Harry'd sent her a particularly lovely message from the Over There (as those people call it) she burst into tears and cried out: 'Oh, why did he never say things like that to me when we were together?'

That was a poser, as they say; I couldn't imagine why he hadn't. Of course I knew it was all wrong and immoral, anyway; but, poor thing, I don't see who it can hurt to help the love-making between a sick woman and a ghost. And I'd taken care to say a Novena against Father Divott finding me out.

Well, I told the poor young man what she wanted to know, and he said: 'Oh, you can tell her an evil influence came between them. Some one who was jealous, and worked against him – here, give me a pencil, and I'll write it out . . .' and he pushed out his hot twitching hand for the paper.

That message fairly made her face burn with joy. 'I knew it – I always knew it!' She flung her thin arms about me, and kissed me. 'Tell me again, Cora, how he said I looked the first day he saw me. . .'

'Why, you must have looked as you look now,' says I to her, 'for there's twenty years fallen from your face.' And so there was.

What helped me to keep on was that she'd grown so much gentler and quieter. Less impatient with the people who waited on her, more understanding with the daughter and Mr. Clingsland. There was a different atmosphere in the house. And sometimes she'd say: 'Cora, there must be poor souls in trouble, with nobody to hold out a hand to them; and I want you to come to me when you run across anybody like that.' So I used to keep that poor young fellow well looked after, and cheered up with little dainties. And you'll never make me believe there was anything wrong in that – or in letting Mrs. Clingsland help me out with the new roof on this house, either.

But there was a day when I found her sitting up in bed when I came in, with two red spots on her thin cheeks. And all the peace had gone out of her poor face. 'Why, Mrs. Clingsland, my dear, what's the matter?' But I could see well enough what it was. Somebody'd been undermining her belief in spirit communications, or whatever they call them, and she'd been crying herself into a fever, thinking I'd made up all I'd told her. 'How do I know you're a medium, anyhow,' she flung out at me with pitiful furious eyes, 'and not taking advantage of me with all this stuff every morning?'

Well, the queer thing was that I took offense at that, not because I was afraid of being found out, but because – heaven help us! – I'd somehow come to believe in that young man Harry and his love-making, and it made me angry to be treated as a fraud. But I kept my temper and my tongue, and went on with the massage as if I hadn't heard her; and she was ashamed to say any more to me. The quarrel between us lasted a week; and then one day, poor soul, she said, whimpering like a drug-taker: 'Cora, I can't get on without the messages you bring me. The ones I get through other people don't sound like Harry – and yours do.'

I was so sorry for her then that I had hard work not to cry with her; but I kept my head, and answered quietly: 'Mrs. Clingsland,

I've been going against my Church, and risking my immortal soul, to get those messages through to you; and if you've found others that can help you, so much the better for me, and I'll go and make my peace with Heaven this very evening,' I said.

'But the other messages don't help me, and I don't want to disbelieve in you,' she sobbed out. 'Only lying awake all night and turning things over, I get so miserable. I shall die if you can't prove to me that it's really Harry speaking to you.'

I began to pack up my things. 'I can't prove that, I'm afraid,' I says in a cold voice, turning away my head so she wouldn't see the tears running down my cheeks.

'Oh, but you must, Cora, or I shall die!' she entreated me; and she looked as if she would, the poor soul.

'How can I prove it to you?' I answered. For all my pity for her, I still resented the way she'd spoken; and I thought how glad I'd be to get the whole business off my soul that very night in the confessional.

She opened her great eyes and looked up at me; and I seemed to see the wraith of her young beauty looking out of them. 'There's only one way,' she whispered.

'Well,' I said, still offended, 'what's the way?'

'You must ask him to repeat to you that letter he wrote, and didn't dare send to me. I'll know instantly then if you're in communication with him, and if you are I'll never doubt you any more.'

Well, I sat down and gave a laugh. 'You think it's as easy as that to talk with the dead, do you?'

'I think he'll know I'm dying too, and have pity on me, and do as I ask.' I said nothing more, but packed up my things and went away.

VI

That letter seemed to me a mountain in my path; and the poor young man, when I told him, thought so too. 'Ah, that's too difficult,' he said. But he told me he'd think it over, and do his best – and I was to come back the next day if I could. 'If only I knew more about her – or about *him*. It's damn difficult, making love for a dead man to a woman you've never seen,' says he with his little cracked laugh. I couldn't deny that it was; but I knew he'd do what he could, and I could see that the difficulty of it somehow spurred him on, while me it only cast down.

So I went back to his room the next evening; and as I climbed the stairs I felt one of those sudden warnings that sometimes used to take me by the throat.

'It's as cold as ice on these stairs,' I thought, 'and I'll wager there's no one made up the fire in his room since morning.' But it wasn't really the cold I was afraid of; I could tell there was worse than that waiting for me.

I pushed open the door and went in. 'Well,' says I, as cheerful as I could, 'I've got a pint of Champagne and a thermos of hot soup for you; but before you get them you've got to tell me –'

He laid there in his bed as if he didn't see me, though his eyes were open; and when I spoke to him he didn't answer. I tried to laugh. 'Mercy!' I says, 'are you so sleepy you can't even look round to see the champagne? Hasn't that slut of a woman been in to 'tend to the Stove for you? The room's as cold as death –' I says, and at the word I stopped short. He neither moved nor spoke; and I felt that the cold came from him, and not from the empty stove. I took hold of his hand, and held the cracked looking-glass to his lips; and I knew he was gone to his Maker. I drew his lids down, and fell on my knees beside the bed. 'You shan't go without a prayer, you poor fellow,' I whispered to him, pulling out my beads.

But though my heart was full of mourning I dursn't pray for long, for I knew I ought to call the people of the house. So I just muttered a prayer for the dead, and then got to my feet again. But before calling in anybody I took a quick look around; for I said to myself it would be better not to leave about any of those bits he'd written down for me. In the shock of finding the poor young man gone I'd clean forgotten all about the letter; but I looked among his few books and papers for anything about the spirit messages, and found nothing. After that I turned back for a last look at him, and a last blessing; and then it was, fallen on the floor and half under the bed, I saw a sheet of paper scribbled over in pencil in his weak writing. I picked it up, and, holy Mother, it was the letter! I hid it away quick in my bag, and I stooped down and kissed him. And then I called the people in.

Well, I mourned the poor young man like a son, and I had a busy day arranging things, and settling about the funeral with the lady that used to befriend him. And with all there was to do I never went near Mrs. Clingsland nor so much as thought of her, that day or the next; and the day after that there was a frantic message, asking what had happened, and saying she was very ill, and I was to come quick, no matter how much else I had to do.

I didn't more than half believe in the illness; I've been about too long among the rich not to be pretty well used to their scares and fusses. But I knew Mrs. Clingsland was just pining to find out if I'd got the letter, and that my only chance of keeping my hold over her was to have it ready in my bag when I went back. And if I didn't keep my hold over her, I knew what slimy hands were waiting in the dark to pull her down.

Well, the labour I had copying out that letter was so great that I didn't hardly notice what was in it; and if I thought about it at all, it was only to wonder if it wasn't worded too plain-like, and if there oughtn't to have been more long words in it, coming from a gentleman to his lady. So with one thing and another I wasn't any too easy in my mind when I appeared again at Mrs. Clingsland's; and if ever I wished myself out of a dangerous job, my dear, I can tell you that was the day...

I went up to her room, the poor lady, and found her in bed, and tossing about, her eyes blazing, and her face full of all the wrinkles I'd worked so hard to rub out of it; and the sight of her softened my heart. After all, I thought, these people don't know what real trouble is; but they've manufactured something so like it that it's about as bad as the genuine thing.

'Well,' she said in a fever, 'well, Cora – the letter? Have you brought me the letter?'

I pulled it out of my bag, and handed it to her; and then I sat down and waited, my heart in my boots. I waited a long time, looking away from her; you couldn't stare at a lady who was reading a message from her sweetheart, could you?

I waited a long time; she must have read the letter very slowly, and then re-read it. Once she sighed, ever so softly; and once she said: 'Oh, Harry, no, no – how foolish' . . . and laughed a little under her breath. Then she was still again for so long that at last I turned my head and took a stealthy look at her. And there she lay on her pillows, the hair waving over them, the letter clasped tight in her hands, and her face smoothed out the way it was years before, when I first knew her. Yes – those few words had done more for her than all my labour.

'Well –?' said I, smiling a little at her.

'Oh, Cora – now at last he's spoken to me, really spoken.' And the tears were running down her young cheeks.

I couldn't hardly keep back my own, the heart was so light in me. 'And now you'll believe in me, I hope, ma'am, won't you?'

'I was mad ever to doubt you, Cora. . .' She lifted the letter to her breast, and slipped it in among her laces. 'How did you manage to get it, you darling, you?'

Dear me, thinks I, and what if she asks me to get her another one like it, and then another? I waited a moment, and then I spoke very gravely. 'It's not an easy thing, ma'am, coaxing a letter like that from the dead.' And suddenly, with a start, I saw that I'd spoken the truth. It *was* from the dead that I'd got it.

'No, Cora; I can well believe it. But this is a treasure I can live on for years. Only you must tell me how I can repay you. . . In a hundred years I could never do enough for you,' she says.

Well, that word went to my heart; but for a minute I didn't know how to answer. For it was true I'd risked my soul, and that was something she couldn't pay me for; but then maybe I'd saved hers, in getting her away from those foul people, so the whole business was more of a puzzle to me than ever. But then I had a thought that made me easier.

'Well, ma'am, the day before yesterday I was with a young man about the age of – of your Harry; a poor young man, without health or hope, lying sick in a mean rooming-house. I used to go there and see him sometimes –'

Mrs. Clingsland sat up in bed in a flutter of pity. 'Oh, Cora, how dreadful! Why did you never tell me? You must hire a better room for him at once. Has he a doctor? Has he a nurse? Quick – give me my cheque-book!'

'Thank you, ma'am. But he don't need no nurse nor no doctor; and he's in a room underground by now. All I wanted to ask you for,' said I at length, though I knew I might have got a king's ransom from her, 'is money enough to have a few masses said for his soul – because maybe there's no one else to do it.'

I had hard work making her believe there was no end to the masses you could say for a hundred dollars; but somehow it's comforted me ever since that I took no more from her that day. I saw to it that Father Divott said the masses and got a good bit of the money; so he was a sort of accomplice too, though he never knew it.

DURATION

I

The passage in his sister's letter most perplexing to Henly Warbeck was that in which she expressed her satisfaction that the date of his sailing from Lima would land him in Boston in good time for cousin Martha Little's birthday.

Puzzle as he would, the returning Bostonian could get no light on it. 'Why,' he thought, after a third re-reading, 'I didn't suppose Martha Little had ever *had* a birthday since the first one!'

Nothing on the fairly flat horizon of Henly Warbeck's youth had been more lacking in relief than the figure of his father's spinster cousin, Martha Little; and now, returning home after many years in distant and exotic lands (during which, however, contact by correspondence had never been long interrupted), Warbeck could not imagine what change in either Martha Little's character or in that of Boston could have thrust her into even momentary prominence.

Even in his own large family connection, where, to his impatient youth, insignificance seemed endemic, Martha Little had always been the most effaced, contourless, colourless. Nor had any accidental advantage ever lifted her out of her congenital twilight: neither money, nor a bad temper, nor a knack with her clothes, nor any of those happy hazards – chance meetings with interesting people, the whim of a rich relation, the luck of ministering in a street accident to somebody with money to bequeath – which occasionally raise the most mediocre above their level. As far as Warbeck knew, Martha Little's insignificance had been unbroken, and accepted from the outset, by herself and all the family, as the medium she was fated to live in: as a person with weak eyes has to live with the blinds down, and be groped for by stumbling visitors.

The result had been that visitors were few; that Martha was more and more forgotten, or remembered only when she could temporarily replace a nursery governess on holiday, or 'amuse' some fidgety child getting over an infantile malady. Then the family took it for granted that she would step into the breach; but when the governess came back, or the child recovered, she disappeared, and was again immediately forgotten.

Once only, as far as Warbeck knew, had she overstepped the line thus drawn for her; but that was so long ago that the occasion had already become a legend in his boyhood. It was when old Mrs. Warbeck, Henly's grandmother, gave the famous ball at which her eldest granddaughter came out; the ball discussed for weeks beforehand and months afterward from Chestnut Street to Bay State Road, not because there was anything exceptional about it (save perhaps its massive 'handsomeness'), but simply because old Mrs. Warbeck had never given a ball before, and Boston had never supposed she ever would give one, and there had been hardly three months' time in which to get used to the idea that she was really going to – at last!

All this, naturally, had been agitating, not to say upsetting, to Beacon Street and Commonwealth Avenue, and absorbing to the whole immense Warbeck connection; the innumerable Pepperels, Sturlisses and Syngletons, the Graysons, Wrigglesworths and Perches – even to those remote and negligible Littles whose name gave so accurate a measure of their tribal standing. And to that ball there had been a question of asking, not of course *all* the Littles – that would have been really out of proportion – but two or three younger specimens of the tribe, whom circumstances had happened to bring into closer contact with the Warbeck group.

'And then,' one of the married daughters had suggested toward the end of the consultation, 'there's Martha Little –'

'*Martha?*' old Mrs. Warbeck echoed, incredulous and ironic, as much as to say: 'The name's a slip of the tongue, of course; but whom *did* you mean, my dear, when you said 'Martha'?'

But the married daughter had continued, though more doubtfully: 'Well, mother, Martha does sometimes help us out of our difficulties. Last winter, you remember, when Maggie's baby had the chickenpox . . . and then, taking Sara's Charlotte three times a week to her drawing-class . . . and you know, as you invite her to stay with you at Milton every summer when we're at the seaside. . .'

'Ah, you regard that as helping you out of a difficulty?' Mrs. Warbeck drily interposed.

'No, mother, not a difficulty, of course. But it does make us feel so *safe* to know that Martha's with you. And when she hears of the ball she might expect –'

'Expect to *come?*' questioned Mrs. Warbeck.

'Oh, no – how absurd! Only to be invited . . .' the daughters chorussed in reply.

'She'd like to show the invitation at her boarding-house. . .'

'She hasn't many pleasures, poor thing. . .'

'Well, but,' the old lady insisted, sticking to her point, 'if I did invite her, would she come?'

'To a ball? What an idea!' Martha Little at a ball! Daughters and daughters-in-law laughed. It was really too absurd. But they all had their little debts to settle with Martha Little, and the opportunity was too good to be missed. On the strength of their joint assurances that no risk could possibly be incurred, old Mrs. Warbeck sent the invitation.

The night of the ball came; and so did Martha Little. She was among the first to arrive, and she stayed till the last candle was blown out. The entertainment remained for many years memorable in the annals of Beacon Street, and also in the Warbeck family history, since it was the occasion of Sara's eldest engaging herself to the second of Jake Wrigglesworth's boys (now, Warbeck reflected, himself a grizzled grandparent), and of Phil Syngleton's falling in love with the second Grayson girl; but beyond and above these events towered the formidable fact of Martha Little's one glaring indelicacy. Like Mrs. Warbeck's ball, it was never repeated. Martha retired once more into the twilight in which she belonged, emerging from it, as of old, only when some service was to be rendered somewhere in the many-branched family connection. But the episode of the ball remained fresh in every memory. Martha Little had been invited – *and she had come*! Henly Warbeck, as a little boy, had often heard his aunts describe her appearance: the prim black silk, the antiquated seed-pearls and lace mittens, the obvious 'front', more tightly crimped than usual; how she had pranced up the illuminated stairs, an absurd velvet reticule over her wrist, greeted her mighty kinswoman on the landing, and complacently mingled with the jewelled and feathered throng under the wax candles of the many chandeliers, while Mrs. Warbeck muttered to her daughters in a withering aside: '*I never should have thought it of Martha Little!*'

The escapade had done Martha Little more harm than good. The following summer Mrs. Warbeck had chosen one of her own granddaughters to keep her company at Milton when the family went to the seaside. It was hoped that this would make Martha realise her fatal error; and it did. And though the following year, at the urgent suggestion of the grand-daughter chosen to replace her, she was received back into grace, and had what she called her 'lovely summer outing' at Milton, there was certainly a shade of difference in her subsequent treatment. The younger granddaughters especially resented the fact that old Mrs. Warbeck had decided never to give another ball;

and the old lady was fond of repeating (before Martha Little) that no, really, she couldn't; the family connection was *too large* – she hadn't room for them all. When the girls wanted to dance, their mothers must hire a public room; at her age Mrs. Warbeck couldn't be subjected to the fatigue, and the – the over-crowding.

Martha Little took the hint. As the grand-children grew up and married, her services were probably less often required, and by the time that Henly Warbeck had graduated from the Harvard Law School, and begun his life of distant wanderings, she had vanished into a still deeper twilight. Only once or twice, when some member of the tribe had run across Henly abroad, had Martha's name been mentioned. 'Oh, she's as dull as Martha Little,' one contemptuous cousin had said of somebody; and the last mention of her had been when Warbeck's sister, Mrs. Pepperel – the one to whom he was now returning – had mentioned, years ago, that a remote Grayson cousin, of the Frostingham branch, had bequeathed to Martha his little house at Frostingham – 'so that now she's off our minds.' And out of our memories, the speaker might have added; for though Frostingham is only a few miles from Boston it was not likely that many visitors would find their way to Martha Little's door.

No; the allusion in this letter of Mrs. Pepperel's remained cryptic to the returning traveller. As the train approached Boston, he pulled it from his pocket, and re-read it again. 'Luckily you'll get here in good time for Martha Little's birthday,' Mrs. Pepperel said.

The train was slowing down. 'Frosting*ham*,' the conductor shouted, stressing the last syllable in the old Boston way. 'Thank heaven,' Warbeck thought, 'nothing ever really changes in Boston!'

A newsboy came through the Pullman with the evening papers. Warbeck unfolded one and read on the first page: 'Frostingham preparing to celebrate Miss Martha Little's hundredth birthday.' And underneath: 'Frostingham's most distinguished centenarian chats with representative of *Transcript*.' But the train was slowing down again – and here was Boston. Warbeck thrust the paper into his suit-case, bewildered yet half-understanding. Where else in the world but in Boston would the fact of having lived to be a hundred lift even a Martha Little into the lime-light? Ah, no; Boston forgot nothing, altered nothing. With a swelling heart the penitent exile sprang out, and was folded to the breasts of a long line of Warbecks and Pepperels, all of whom congratulated him on having arrived from the ends of the earth in time for Martha Little's birthday.

II

That night after dinner, Warbeck leaned back at ease in the pleasant dining-room of the old Pepperel house in Chestnut Street. The Copley portraits looked down familiarly from the walls, the old Pepperel Madeira circulated about the table. (In New York, thought Warbeck, Copleys and Madeiras, if there had been any, would both have been sold long since.)

The atmosphere was warm to the returning wanderer. It was pleasant to see about him the animated replicas of the Copleys on the walls, and to listen again to the local intonations, with the funny stress on the last syllable. His unmarried Pepperel nieces were fresh and good-looking; and the youngest, Lyddy, judging from her photograph, conspicuously handsome. But Lyddy was not there. Cousin Martha, Mrs. Pepperel explained with a certain pride, was so fond of Lyddy that the girl had to be constantly with her; and since the preparations for the hundredth birthday had begun, Lyddy had been virtually a prisoner at Frostingham. 'Martha wouldn't even let her off to come and dine with you tonight; she says she's too nervous and excited to be left without Lyddy. Lyddy is my most self-sacrificing child,' Mrs. Pepperel added complacently. One of the younger daughters laughed.

'Cousin Martha says she's going to leave Lyddy her seed-pearls!'

'Priscilla –!' her mother rebuked her.

'Well, mother, they *are* beauties.'

'I should say they were,' Mrs. Pepperel bridled. 'The old Wrigglesworth seed-pearls – simply priceless. Martha's been offered anything for them! All I can say is, if my child gets them, she's deserved it.'

Warbeck reflected. 'Were they the funny old ornaments that everybody laughed at when Martha wore them at Grandma Warbeck's famous ball?'

His sister wrinkled her brows. 'That wonderful ball of Grandma's? Did Martha wear them there, I wonder – all those centuries ago? I suppose then that nobody appreciated them,' she murmured.

Warbeck felt as if he were in a dream in which everything happens upside-down. He was listening to his sister's familiar kind of family anecdote, told in familiar words and in a familiar setting; but the Family Tyrant, once named with mingled awe and pride, was no longer the all-powerful Grandma Warbeck of his childhood, but her effaced imperceptible victim, Martha Little. Warbeck listened sympathetically, yet he felt an underlying constraint. His sister obviously thought he lacked interest in the Frostingham celebrations, and even her husband, whose mental processes were so slow and subterranean that they never altered his motionless countenance, was heard to mutter: 'Well, I don't suppose many families can produce a brace of centenarians in one year.'

'A brace –?' Warbeck laughed, while the nieces giggled, and their mother looked suddenly grave.

'You know, Grayson, I've never approved of the Perches forcing themselves in.' She turned to Warbeck. 'You've been away so long that you won't understand; but I do think it shows a lack of delicacy in the Perches.'

'Why, what have they done?' Warbeck asked; while the nieces' giggles grew uncontrollable.

'Dragged an old Perch great-uncle out of goodness knows where, on the pretext that *he's* a hundred too. Of course we never heard a word of it till your aunts and I decided to do something appropriate about Martha Little. And how do we know he *is* a hundred?'

'Sara!' her husband interjected.

'Well, I think we ought to have asked for an affidavit before a notary. Crowding in at the eleventh hour! Why, Syngleton Perch doesn't even live in Massachusetts. Why don't they have *their* centenary in Rhode Island? Because they know nobody'd go to it – that's why!'

'Sara, the excitement's been too much for you,' said Mr. Pepperel judicially.

'Well, I believe it will be, if this sort of thing goes on. Girls, are you sure there are programmes enough? Come – we'd better go up to the drawing-room and go over the list again.' She turned affectionately to her brother. 'It'll make all the difference to Martha, your being here. She was so excited when she heard you were coming. You've got to sit on the platform next to her – or next but one. Of course she must be between the Senator and the Bishop. Syngleton Perch wanted to crowd into the third place; but it's yours, Martha says; and of course when Martha says a thing, that settles it!'

'Medes and Persians,' muttered Mr. Pepperel, with a wink which did not displace his features; but his wife interposed: 'Grayson, you know I hate your saying disrespectful things about Martha!'

Warbeck went to bed full of plans for the next day: old friends to be looked up, the Museums to be seen, and a tramp out on the Mill Dam, down the throat of a rousing Boston east wind. But these invigorating plans were shattered by an early message from Frostingham. Cousin Martha Little expected Warbeck to come and see her; he was to lunch early and be at Frostingham at two sharp. And he must not fail to be punctual, for before her afternoon nap cousin Martha was to have a last fitting of her dress for the ceremony.

'You'd think it was her wedding dress!' Warbeck ventured jocosely; but Mrs. Pepperel received the remark without a smile. 'Martha is *very* wonderful,' she murmured; and her brother acquiesced: 'She must be.'

At two sharp his car drew up before the little old Grayson house. On the way out to Frostingham the morning papers had shown him photographs of its pilastered front, and a small figure leaning on a stick between the elaborate door-lights. 'Two Relics of a Historic Past,' the headline ran.

Warbeck, guided by the radiant Lyddy, was led into a small square parlour furnished with the traditional Copleys and mahogany. He perceived that old Grayson's dingy little house had been an unsuspected treasury of family relics; and enthroned among them sat the supreme relic, the Crown Jewel of the clan.

'You don't recognise your cousin Martha!' shrilled a small reedy voice, and a mummied hand shot out of its lace ruffles with a slight upward tilt which Warbeck took as hint to salute it. The hand tasted like an old brown glove that had been kept in a sandal-wood box.

'Of course I know you, cousin Martha. You're not changed the least little bit!'

She lifted from her ruffles a small mottled face like a fruit just changing into a seed-pod. Her expression was obviously resentful. 'Not changed? Then you haven't noticed the new way I do my hair?'

The challenge disconcerted Warbeck. 'Well, you know, it's a long time since we met – going on for thirty years,' he bantered.

'Thirty years?' She wrinkled her brows. 'When I was as young as that I suppose I still wore a pompadour!'

When she was as young – as seventy! Warbeck felt like a gawky school-boy. He was at a loss what to say next; but the radiant Lyddy gave him his clue. 'Cousin Martha was so delighted when she heard you were coming all the way from Peru on purpose for her Birthday.' Her eyes met his with such a look of liquid candour that he saw she believed in the legend herself.

'Well, I don't suppose many of the family have come from farther off than I have,' he boasted hypocritically.

Miss Little tilted up her chin again. 'Did you fly?' she snapped; and without waiting for his answer: 'I'm going to fly this summer. I wanted to go up before my birthday; it would have looked well in the papers. But the weather's been too unsettled.'

It would have looked well in the papers! Warbeck listened to her, stupefied. Was it the old Martha Little speaking? There was something changed in Boston, after all. But she began to glance nervously toward the door. 'Lyddy, I think I heard the bell.'

'I'll go and see, cousin Martha.'

Miss Little sank back into her cushions with a satisfied smile. 'These reporters –!'

'Ah – you think it's an interview?'

She pursed up her unsteady slit of a mouth. 'As if I hadn't told them everything already! It's all coming out in the papers tomorrow. Haven't touched wine or black coffee for forty years. . . Light massage every morning; very light supper at six. . . I cleaned out the canary's cage myself every day till last December. . . Oh, and I *love* my Sunday sermon on the wireless. . . But they won't leave a poor old woman in peace. 'Miss Little, won't you give us your views on President Coolidge – or on companionate marriage?' I suppose this one wants to force himself in for the rehearsal.'

'The rehearsal?'

She pursed up her mouth again. 'Sara Pepperel didn't tell you? Such featherheads, all those Pepperels! Even Lyddy – though she's a good child. . . I'm to try on my dress at three; and after that, just a little informal preparation for the ceremony. The Frostingham selectmen are to present me with a cane . . . a gold-headed cane with an inscription . . . *Lyddy*!' Her thread of a voice rose in a sudden angry pipe.

Lyddy thrust in a flushed and anxious face. 'Oh, cousin Martha –'

'Well, *is* it a reporter? What paper? Tell him, if he'll promise to sit perfectly quiet. . .'

'It's not a reporter, cousin Martha. It's – it's cousin Syngleton Perch. He says he wants to pay you his respects: and he thinks he ought to take part in the rehearsal. Now please don't excite yourself, cousin Martha!'

'Excite myself, child? Syngleton Perch can't steal my birthday, can he? If he chooses to assist at it – after all, the Perches are our own people; his mother was a Wrigglesworth.' Miss Little drew herself up by the arms of her chair. 'Show your cousin Syngleton in, my dear.'

On the threshold a middle-aged motherly voice said, rather loudly: 'This way, uncle Syngleton. You won't take my arm? Well, then put your stick *there*; so – this way; careful . . .' and there tottered in, projected forward by a series of jaunty jerks, and the arm of his unseen guide, a small old gentleman in a short pea-jacket, with a round withered head buried in layers of woollen scarf, and eyes hidden behind a huge pair of black spectacles.

'Where's my old friend Martha Little? Now, then, Marty, don't you try and hide yourself away from young Syngleton. Ah, there she is! *I* see her!' cousin Syngleton rattled out in a succession of parrotlike ejaculations, as his elderly Antigone and the young Lyddy steered him cautiously toward Miss Little's throne.

From it she critically observed the approach of the rival centenarian; and as he reached her side, and stretched out his smartly-gloved hand, she dropped hers into it with a faint laugh. 'Well, you really *are* a hundred, Syngleton Perch; there's no doubt about that,' she said in her high chirp. 'And I wonder whether you haven't postponed your anniversary a year or two?' she added with a caustic touch, and a tilt of her chin toward Warbeck.

III

Transporting centenarians from one floor to another was no doubt a delicate business, for the vigilant Lyddy had staged the trying-on of the ceremonial dress in the dining-room, where the rehearsal was also to take place. Miss Little withdrew, and cousin Syngleton Perch's watchful relative, having installed him in an armchair facing Warbeck's as carefully as if she had been balancing a basket of eggs on a picket fence, slipped off with an apologetic smile to assist at the trying-on. 'I know you'll take care of him, cousin Henly,' she murmured in a last appeal; and added, bending to Warbeck's ear: 'Please remember he's a little deaf; and don't let him get too excited talking about his love-affairs.'

Uncle Syngleton, wedged in tightly with cushions, and sustained by a footstool, peered doubtfully at Warbeck as the latter held out his cigarette-case. 'Tobacco? Well . . . look here, young man, what paper do you represent?' he asked, his knotty old hand yearningly poised above the coveted cigarette.

Warbeck explained in a loud voice that he was not a journalist, but a member of the family; but Mr. Perch shook his head incredulously. 'That's what they all say; worming themselves in everywhere. Plain truth is, I never saw you before, nor you me. But see here; we may have to wait an hour while that young charmer gets into her party togs, and I don't know's I can hold out that long without a puff of tobacco.' He shot a wrinkled smile at Warbeck. 'Time was when I'd'a been in there myself, assisting at the dish-abille.' (He pronounced the first syllable *dish*.) A look of caution replaced his confidential smirk. 'Well, young man,

I suppose what you want is my receipt for keeping hale and hearty up to the century line. But there's nothing new about it: it's just the golden rule of good behaviour that our mothers taught us in the nursery. No wine, no tobacco, no worn – . Well,' he broke off, with a yearning smile at the cigarette-case, 'I don't mind if I do. Got a light, young gentleman? Though if I *was* to assist at an undressing, I don't say,' he added meditatively, 'that it'd be Martha Little's I'd choose. I remember her when she warn't over thirty – too much like a hygienic cigarette even then, for my fancy. De-nicotinised, I call her. Well, I like the unexpurgated style better.' He held out his twitching hand to Warbeck's lighter, and inserted a cigarette between his purplish lips. 'Some punch in that! Only don't you give me away, will you? Not in the papers, I mean. Remember old Syngleton Perch's slogan: 'Live straight and you'll live long. No wine, no tobacco, no worn –'. Again he broke off, and thumped his crumpled fist excitedly against the chair-arm. 'Damn it, sir, I never *can* finish that lie, somehow! Old Syngleton a vestal? Not if I know anything about him!'

The door opened, and Lyddy and the motherly Antigone showed their flushed faces. 'Now then, uncle Syngleton – all ready!'

They were too much engrossed to notice Warbeck, but he saw that his help was welcome, for extricating Syngleton from his armchair was like hooking up a broken cork which, at each prod, slips down farther into the neck of the bottle. Once on his legs he goose-stepped valiantly forward; but until he had been balanced on them he tended to fold up at the very moment when his supporters thought they could prudently release him.

The transit accomplished, Warbeck found himself in a room from which the dining-table had been removed to make way for an improvised platform supporting a row of armchairs.

In the central armchair Martha Little, small and hieratic, sat enthroned. About her billowed the rich folds of a silvery shot-silk, and the Wrigglesworth seed-pearls hung over her hollow chest and depended from her dusky withered ears. A row of people sat facing her, at the opposite end of the room, and Warbeck noticed that two or three already had their pens in leash above open notebooks. A strange young woman of fashionable silhouette was stooping over the shot-silk draperies and ruffling them with a professional touch. 'Isn't she too old-world for anything? Just the Martha Washington note: isn't it lovely, with her pearls? Please note: *The Wrigglesworth pearls*, Miss Lusky,' she recommended to a zealous reportress with suspended pen.

'Now, whatever you do, don't shake me!' snapped the shot-silk divinity, as Syngleton and his supporters neared the platform. ('It's the powder in her hair she's nervous about,' Lyddy whispered to Warbeck.)

The business of raising the co-divinity to her side was at once ticklish and laborious, for Mr. Perch resented feminine assistance in the presence of strange men, and Warbeck, even with the bungling support of one of the journalists, found it difficult to get his centenarian relative hoisted to the platform. Any attempt to lift him caused his legs to shoot upward, and to steady and direct this levitating tendency required an experience in which both assistants were lacking.

'*There!*' his household Antigone intervened, seizing one ankle while Lyddy clutched the other; and thus ballasted Syngleton Perch recovered his powers of self-direction and made for the armchair on Miss Little's right. At his approach she uttered a shrill cry and tried to raise herself from her seat.

'No, no! This is the Bishop's!' she protested, defending the chair with her mittened hand.

'Oh, my – there go all the folds of her skirt,' wailed the dress-maker from the background.

Syngleton Perch stood on the platform and his bullet head grew purple. 'Can't stand – got to sit down or keep going,' he snapped.

Martha Little subsided majestically among her disordered folds. 'Well – keep going!' she decreed.

'Oh, cousin Martha,' Lyddy murmured.

'Well, what of cousin Martha? It's *my* rehearsal, isn't it?' the lady retorted, like a child whimpering for a toy.

'Cousin Martha – cousin *Martha*!' Lyddy whispered, while Syngleton, with flickering legs, protested: 'Don't I belong anywhere in this show?' and Warbeck caught Lyddy's warning murmur: 'Don't forget, cousin Martha, *his mother was a Wrigglesworth*!'

As if by magic Miss Little's exasperation gave way to a resigned grimace. '*He* says so,' she muttered sulkily; but the appeal to the great ancestral name had not been vain, and she suffered her rival to be established in the armchair just beyond the Bishop's, while his guide, hovering over his shoulder, announced to the journalists: 'Mr. Syngleton Perch, of South Perch, Rhode Island, whose hundredth birthday will be celebrated with that of his cousin Miss Little tomorrow –'

'H'm – *tomorrow*!' Miss Little suddenly exclaimed, again attempting to rise from her throne; while Syngleton's staccato began to unroll the automatic phrase: 'I suppose you young men all want to know my receipt for keeping hale and hearty up to the century line. Well, there's nothing new about it: it's just the golden rule . . . the . . . what the devil's *that?*' he broke off with a jerk of his chin toward the door.

Warbeck saw that an object had been handed into the room by a maid, and was being passed from hand to hand up to the platform. 'Oh,' Lyddy exclaimed breathlessly, 'of course! It's the ebony cane! The Selectmen have sent it up for cousin Martha to try today, so that she'll be sure it was just right for her to lean on when she walks out of the Town Hall tomorrow after the ceremony. Look what a beauty it is – you'll let these gentlemen look at it, won't you, cousin Martha?'

'If they can look at me I suppose they can look at my cane,' said Miss Little imperially, while the commemorative stick was passed about the room amid admiring exclamations, and attempts to decipher its laudatory inscription. ' 'Offered to Frostingham's most beloved and distinguished citizen, Martha Wrigglesworth Little, in commemoration of the hundredth anniversary of her birth, by her friends the Mayor and Selectmen' . . . very suitable, very interesting,' an elderly cousin read aloud with proper emotion, while Mr. Perch was heard to enquire anxiously: 'Isn't there anything about me on that cane?' and his companion reassured him: 'Of course South Perch means to offer you one of your very own when we go home.'

Finally the coveted object was restored to Miss Little, who, straightening herself with a supreme effort, sat resting both hands on the gold crutch while Lyddy hailed the approach of imaginary dignitaries with the successive announcements: 'The Bishop – the Mayor. . . But, no, they'd better be seated before you arrive, hadn't they, cousin Martha? And exactly *when* is the cane to be presented? Oh, well, we'll settle all the details to-morrow . . . the main thing now is the stepping down from the platform and walking out of the Hall, isn't it? Miss Lusky, careful, please. . . Gentlemen, will you all move your chairs back? . . . Uncle Henly,' she appealed to Warbeck, 'perhaps you'll be kind enough to act as Mayor, and give your arm to cousin Martha? Ready, cousin Martha? So –'

But as she was about to raise Miss Little from her seat, and hook her securely onto Warbeck's arm, a cry between a sob and an expletive burst from the purple lips of cousin Syngleton.

'Why can't *I* be the Mayor – ain't I got any rights in this damned show?' he burst out passionately, his legs jerking upward as he attempted to raise himself on his elbows.

His Antigone intervened with a reproachful murmur. 'Why, uncle Syngleton, what in the world are you thinking of? You can't act as anybody but *yourself* tomorrow! But I'm going to be the Bishop now, and give you my arm – there, like this. . .'

Miss Little, who had just gained her feet, pressed heavily on Warbeck's arm in her effort to jerk around toward Mr. Perch. 'Oh, he's going to take the Bishop's arm, is he? Well, the Bishop had better look out, or he'll take his seat too,' she chuckled ironically.

Cousin Syngleton turned a deeper purple. 'Oh, I'll take his seat too, will I? Well, why not? Isn't this my anniversary as much as it is yours, Martha Little? I suppose you think I'd better follow after you and carry your train, eh?'

Miss Little drew herself up to a height that seemed to overshadow every one around her. Warbeck felt her shaking on his arm like a withered leaf, but her lips were dangerously merry.

'No; I think you'd better push the Mayor out of the way and give *me* your arm, Syngleton Perch,' she flung back gaily.

'Well, why not?' Mr. Perch rejoined, his innocent smile meeting her perfidious one; and some one among the lookers-on was imprudent enough to exclaim: 'Oh, wouldn't that be too lovely!'

'Oh, uncle Syngleton,' Lyddy appealed to him – 'do you really suppose you *could?*'

'Could – could – could, young woman? Who says I can't, I'd like to know?' uncle Syngleton sputtered, his arms and legs gyrating vehemently toward Miss Little, who now stood quite still on Warbeck's arm, the cane sustaining her, and her fixed smile seeming to invite her rival's approach.

'An interesting experiment,' Warbeck heard some one mutter in the background, and Miss Little's head turned in the direction of the speaker. 'This is only a rehearsal,' she declared incisively.

She remained motionless and untrembling while the Antigone and Lyddy guided cousin Syngleton precariously toward her;

but just as Warbeck thought she was about to detach her hand from his arm, and transfer her frail weight to Mr. Perch's, she made an unexpected movement. Its immediate result – Warbeck could never say how – was to shoot forward the famous ebony stick which her abrupt gesture (was it unconsciously?) drove directly into the path of uncle Syngleton. In another instant – but one instant too late for rescue – Warbeck saw the stick entangled in the old man's wavering feet, and beheld him shoot wildly upward, and then fall over with a crash. Every one in the room gathered about with agitated questions and exclamations, struggling to lift him to his feet; only Miss Little continued to stand apart, her countenance unmoved, her aged fingers still imbedded in Warbeck's arm.

The old man, prone and purple, was being cautiously lifted down from the platform, while the bewildered spectators parted, awe-struck, to make way for his frightened bearers. Warbeck followed their movements with alarm; then he turned anxiously toward the frail figure on his arm. How would she bear the shock, he asked himself, with a leap of the imagination which seemed to lay her also prone at his feet. But she stood upright, unmoved, and Warbeck met her resolute eyes with a start, and saw in their depths a century of slow revenge.

'Oh, cousin Martha – cousin *Martha*,' he breathed, in a whisper of mingled terror and admiration...

'Well, what? I told you it was only a rehearsal,' said Martha Little, with her ancient smile.